The Merchant

A Story Only Told to a Few...

JV Author Services Edition – UK

The Merchant
.... *A Story Only Told to a Few...*

JV Author Services Edition – UK
www.jvauthorservices.co.uk

ISBN 978-1-7392970-3-9

Cover Design: Floss Design
Book editing & Formatting: JV Author Services

www.ukinkers.com

Dedication

To

Dame Dominique
Natalie – counting stars together
Dr Hala Banna
Dr Youssreya Abou-Hadid

&

My Mother

Special Thanks

My Family

John & Vicky Regan
JV Author Services

Kirsty McKay & Team

Lubna Salem

Karim Hassan & 88 Team

Join UK inkers

We aim to gather the people required for a successful publisher in one meeting point. Of course, we start with the writers and connect them with publishers, editors, agents, bookstores, book designers, filmmakers, PR & marketing experts, and even logistical and payment solution providers.

How does it work?

Authors send us their work. Then we feature authors we find offering an addition to the literary scene. Interested publishers and agents approach them, and authors contact editors, book designers or whomever they need to get their books to the scene. And then, it all begins, and we add authors to the scene and enrich the literature further.

Whom are we starting with?

Extraordinary authors and whoever is ready to step out of the mainstream and join our community that works for the benefit of the Word, whether written in ink or pixels.

Why focus on the UK?

It is the capital of literature and the royal court of authors.

www.ukinkers.com

About the Author

Born in 1978 in London –the UK, then moved to Cairo, Egypt, in the early 1980s.

He started writing poetry in school, and during college, he won first prize in the English poetry contest for three consecutive years.

Also, during college, he became co-head of the poetry club in Egypt's best-selling English magazine.

After graduating in computer & management sciences, he joined Nile TV international as an editor, then moved up to be an editor-in-chief, reporter and news anchor.

He later used his creative and writing skills in public relations, advertisement, marketing, and copyrighting.

After spending six years writing his first novel, he sent the manuscript to Her Majesty the Queen to reward himself morally.

After successfully publishing his novel in Egypt, he founded Ukinkers.com to publish 'The Merchant' in the UK.

Sherif El Hotabiy

Introduction

We are about to share the same feeling, so thank you for reading my book.

Sherif.

Prologue

The Merchant

Every drop of every sea has touched one of my boats,
Travelling the world with my fleet,
Every sand of every shore has felt my boots,
Stomping the lands with my feet,
Eyes wide open and bold,
Careless to summer heat and winter cold,
Untouchable by no burglar nor pirate,
In the presence of mine,
Guns grow silent,
With every sunset and sunrise,
I bought and sold merchandise,
Until I saw that one beautiful woman,
For only she looks like one, I say she is human,
It is your heart,
That I want,
What price should I pay in gold, silver, or brass?
Words, vows or maybe love filled in a crystal glass,
I will not look for an answer,
Will not wait any longer,
I walked over the fire, water, mud, and ice,
And I know hearts have no price,
True love is the worst thing at which a man would fail, Attention
sailors, Pull up the anchors, And set sail … set sail.

Chapter 1

One step at a time, the sailor thought to himself as he made his way along the seashore – his feet heavy and his head dizzy. He had started walking the shore at the break of dawn, but now it was noon. Yes, noon. Indeed, the scorching sun sat right above his head. With nearly open eyes, he looked at it, well, almost did, as the sweat ran down his forehead. Needing to rest for a while, he slid his backpack off his shoulder. Walking a couple of steps into the sea, he dropped to his knees, took off his sailor hat, soaked it in the salty sea water, and put it back on. Trying to cool off, he splashed his face with water and sighed while taking a deep look at the horizon. *Waves, just waves, one after another, like steps, one after another. Where to? Where are my steps leading me? Somewhere ... it must lead somewhere ... or should I keep walking pointlessly, just like those waves to the shore and back, and again, to the shore and back? Waves, minutes, days, years ... steps ... all to the shore and back. Is there any point to all of this?*

Then it came into sight. To his left, a lighthouse loomed in the distance. He pulled his backpack onto his shoulders and sunk his ankles back in the sand as he started to walk again, but this time towards the lighthouse. Drained, he walked one step at a time ... steadily ... one step at a time.

He finally reached the lighthouse and stared at it. It looked like any other lighthouse he had seen before, but this one was much older than any he had encountered previously. It looked ancient, standing high at the end of a rocky land formation that stretched into the sea – the waves crashing onto its sides.

He pulled his shoes out of his backpack, pushed them on, and made for the lighthouse. It was a slightly refreshing walk as waves splashed on both sides, rhythmically, one after another, until he reached the door. He thought of knocking, but the wooden door was cracked, and the doorknob rusted, so it occurred to him that it might be deserted. He gently opened the door – a loud squeak announced his arrival just before he said, "Hello."

After walking in the sun for hours, his eyes struggled inside the lighthouse. "Hello," he repeated in a louder voice, but still, no one answered. A moment later, with his eyes now adjusted to the shadowiness, he spotted the stairwell – rusty and silent.

He peered up the stairs. *Maybe there is someone up there,* he thought. *If not, it could be a place to rest for a while away from the savage sun.* With cautious steps, he spiralled his way upwards.

At the top, a circular chamber of grey stone bricks met him, with a wide glass window that encircled the main lamp. A massive and powerful lamp that the lighthouse keeper switched on and rotated at night to guide sailing ships to shore. Though he had never been inside a lighthouse before, it was as he expected. He glanced around and spotted an older man sitting on a chair facing the sea, his head tilted backwards and his legs outstretched. His arms were hanging down by his sides as if he had thrown his body into the chair.

The sailor stepped closer. The man wore a thick grey wool jacket – that just didn't fit the weather – navy blue trousers, black boots, a white t-shirt, and a dark grey hat that showed a little of his entirely white hair. *Was he the lighthouse keeper?* He mused. *He must be.*

"Hello," the sailor said, but the man didn't answer, turn his head, or move an inch. The sailor slowly approached the man and examined his deeply wrinkled face. The old keeper's eyes were shut, and his mouth open. *Was he asleep?*

The sailor stepped backwards quietly and was about to turn away. *Maybe I should leave, carry on, or maybe ...* But as he turned, his backpack knocked a cast iron teapot off the shelf and sent it banging to the floor.

"Huh ... what? Who? ... who ... you?" the old keeper said.

"Easy," the sailor said, and held up his hands, palms facing forward. "Easy," he repeated.

The older man attempted to stand, but, losing his balance, he slumped to the floor.

The sailor rushed to him. "I am just a sailor ... calm down, I am just a sailor."

The older man rubbed the sleep from his eyes. "What are you doing here? What do you want?"

"I ... I was walking the shore, just passing by. I needed to stop. I've been walking the shore for a long time. I was looking for somewhere to rest and shelter from the sun. I meant no harm. I thought this place was deserted."

The older man scrutinised the young sailor's face and smiled, nodding slowly. "What's your name?"

The sailor took a deep breath, exhaled slowly and sat on the floor. "I am a sailor. Just a sailor, old mate."

Chapter 2

The water boiled inside the pot. The old keeper stood in front of it, staring at the rolling water, then picked it up with a worn, damp piece of grey cloth.

The sailor sat silently on a wooden chair a couple of feet from the old man and stared through the window at the horizon. It was getting cloudy now, and the winds were picking up.

The old keeper filled two tin cups with tea, handed one to the sailor, and then sat on the chair opposite him. "You are walking the shore, huh?"

"Yes, I am."

"For how long now?"

The sailor sneered. "Long enough to reach this stranded place."

The old keeper pointed at the sailor's clothes and backpack. "You are a sailor then?"

The sailor smiled. "Aye."

The old keeper sipped his tea as the two men appraised each other.

"This is good," the sailor said, nodding at his cup. "Very good." He looked at the tea. "What tea is it?"

"From the Far East."

"I've never tasted tea like it." He surveyed his surroundings. "How long have you lived here, if I may ask? Are you living here? There is no village close enough to come back and forth to, so I figured you must be. Am I right?"

"Yes. I've lived here for a long time on this stranded shore – long enough to lose track of time," the old keeper said, then added, "I bet you are short on supplies? Walking all this way, you must need food and fresh water?" He pointed to the sailor's backpack.

The sailor nodded. "I've almost run out."

The old keeper rested his teacup on the table, eased himself from his chair and took the almost empty water bottles the sailor now held up.

The old keeper opened the bottles, rattled a dull silver coin out of each, and then opened a small drawer filled with shiny silver coins. "Shiny new ones will keep your water fresh better than those rusted coins." He dropped one in each bottle and filled them with fresh water out of a large wooden barrel.

"Where do you keep your water?"

The old keeper pointed above him. "Up there," he said, "and when the clouds dry up, I borrow from ships passing by." He filled the last bottle, resealed it, and handed them to the sailor, along with three cans of food, sea biscuits, and three full water bottles.

The sailor thanked him and stuffed the items into his bag.

"You are a well-mannered sailor," the old keeper said, "but you have foolishly risked your life coming all the way here on just a couple of water bottles. So tell me, how did you get lost?"

"I am not lost, old mate. Who said anything about me being lost?"

"No one has to say anything. You are a sailor who walks the shore, so you must be lost."

The sailor shook his head. "No. I am not."

"So why are you off your ship? Why are you walking on the shore? Look at the world, son. It is made of land and sea. Some farm the land, some sail the sea, but only the lost ones walk the shore."

The sailor rubbed his chin.

The old keeper raised his eyebrows. "What is your story?" He sat. "Is it a long one?"

The sailor looked away. "I don't have one."

"That can't be. Everyone has a story to keep, a story to tell, or a story to live."

"Some lives are too simple to be a story."

The old keeper chuckled. "Life is too great to be simple."

"Well, maybe mine is simple," the sailor said, turning to face the older man. "What about yours? You can't grow as old as you without having a story." The old keeper sat motionless. "Well?" the sailor persisted and glanced outside at the waves smashing onto the rocks sending spray high in the air.

The old keeper laced his hands together. "They say every lighthouse keeper receives one last visitor to hear his story before he is done."

The sailor laughed. "Oh, you think I am here to listen to your story?"

The old keeper narrowed his eyes. "Yes."

"Well, it seems I have to stay here for a while. It looks like a storm is on its way." He pointed out of the window to the grey-clouded sky. "So go on, tell it to me."

"My story isn't mine," the old keeper said. "It isn't about me."

"Not about you?" The sailor laughed again. "What is it about then? I hope it is not about another sea monster."

The old keeper leant forward. "No, not a sea monster. A sea master."

Chapter 3

The old keeper placed his empty cup aside. "My story begins a long time ago. Somewhere on the sea, a ship sailed early in the morning …

… The ship's captain, wearing his full naval uniform, locked himself in his cabin, unrolled a map, pinned it on a wooden table, and studied it thoroughly. His cabin was exceptional. Complete with full crystal wear in his closet and an impressive mini candle chandelier hanging in the middle of the ornate wooden ceiling. The crystals whispered their clinks as the ship rocked its way through the waves. Having given orders not to be disturbed, he groaned when someone knocked on his door.

'Pardon me, captain,' a voice came from the outside.

The captain recognised his first mate. 'What is it?'

'We need you on deck, sir.'

The captain, still leaning over the map, growled. 'Is it an emergency?'

'Not exactly … captain … but …'

'Then do not disturb me, as I commanded.'

'Captain … it is …' the first mate mumbled behind the door. 'Captain, I think we are being followed.'

The captain marched to the door and pulled it open. 'What are you saying?'

'A ship has been straight on our stern for a while now, captain.'

He sighed. 'So? They could be lost and following us for help. It happens, doesn't it?'

'In that case, we would have known who they are, captain.'

'What do you mean?'

'They are hoisting no flags,' the first mate explained, then added, 'They could be pirates, sir.'

The captain pushed past his first mate and hurried towards the stern, closely followed by his junior. He opened his telescope and scrutinised the vessel through the mist. 'That ship?' he said.

'Aye, captain.'

'She seems pretty far from us,' the captain said. 'They are no threat.' He folded his telescope.

The first mate pointed to the ship. 'But they are not hoisting any flags.'

The captain took a deep breath, exhaled, and turned to the first mate. 'I understand that this is the first time you have sailed under my command, and you are not quite acquainted with my methods, but answer me this, are they hoisting a pirates' flag?'

The first mate looked down. 'No, captain.'

'Then, from now on, please do me the courtesy of not jumping to conclusions and follow my orders strictly. I said I did not want to be disturbed, and I don't from now on. Understood?'

'Aye, captain.'

The captain marched back below deck, leaving the first mate looking at the other ship in the distance. He reached his cabin, slammed the door behind him, sat and exhaled a deep breath, then refocused on the map he had himself drawn up. He was an exceptional cartographer, and his reputation as a mapping genius was well-known. His charts meticulously laboured over, more accurate than any other.

He continued his work – refining every edge, every line, and every corner of the map. He used the tools available, marked every spot and even marked a calendar sail on the map, which shows the sailing lines best taken around the seasons.

It took a while – an hour or so – of extreme focus. His head felt heavy, so he thought of taking a break or maybe a nap, but his thoughts were interrupted again, this time not by a knock on the door. It wasn't a voice. Instead, it was a noise, a boom, then a splash. It sounded far away, but then there was a louder boom and a closer splash. His eyes widened as realisation dawned on him. The boom and splash could only mean one thing – cannonballs. Someone was firing at his ship. He hastened from his cabin and headed upwards.

On deck, the captain rushed to the first mate at the helm, who was using all his strength to manoeuvre the ship to safety.

Sailors rushed around, climbing up and down rigging and opening the masts for the ship to pick up speed. Although the crew were trained and experienced, they panicked as the ship approached them at speed. The ship following them was indeed a pirates' ship …

"I don't get it," the sailor interrupted the old keeper, "you said they were all panicking, right?"

"Yes," the old keeper replied.

"It wasn't their first battle. I mean, all, or at least most of them, had been through battles before. They could be frightened at most, but panicking sounds a little too much, doesn't it?"

"True," the old keeper said. "Almost all had seen battles before and fought well. But at those times, cannons were placed on the ship's sides, mainly on the middle and lower decks. Guns were pushed through hatches that were only open to fire, and ships that shot first or had more docks to place more cannons won. Ships had to attack sideways and only sideways. This was how the battles went. But this time, the attack was different." …

… The pirates' vessel had placed two cannons at the tip of the ship, and they were following the captain's ship. The pirates fired at them from behind, so the captain couldn't retaliate. Their only chance was to outrun them, turn sideways and fire back at the pirates. The pirates piled cannon balls in the middle of the main deck to balance the weight of the two heavy cannons at the bow of their ship. They rolled one cannonball after the other to the bow to reload the cannons and fire.

'They are closing in,' one of the sailors yelled as he watched the pirates' ship narrow the gap.

The captain saw that what they were doing wasn't working. The manoeuvring was failing, slowing the ship down, and the pirates would board his ship sooner rather than later. They needed to run or hide. Instinctively he looked around for a getaway, and there it was, clouds of advection fog right above the waters. He took the helm from the first mate and ordered him, 'Get a dozen men to bring me a cannon from the lower deck and place it at the stern right now!'

The first mate hesitated, 'Captain?'

'Now!' the captain shouted. The first mate rushed to execute the order as the captain directed the ship into the fog, into the mist, hoping that the pirates might miss their target enough times needed to reach the fog. He sailed straight, windward, to gain some speed, and get deep enough into the mist to turn and fire back. Air filled up the masts and lifted the ship's bow as it gained momentum and headed straight into the fog.

In the lower deck, twelve cannons were lined up, six on each side, heavy guns of a black alloy metal, each resting on a two-wheeled wooden base and chained to the floor. One man was in charge of them. He maintained them carefully and readied them for battle. Everyone trusted him with their lives and depended on his meticulous dedication, so he stood fast in his post, down in the shade. He rarely ever stood in broad sunlight, and because of this, his face stayed pale.

'Pale Face,' one of the dozen men called out, rushing down the stairs to the lower deck, or as they called it, the fire floor.

'We need a cannon on the main deck, captain's orders!'

'What? Now? How?' Pale Face seemed confused.

The cannon balls firing at the ship continued to echo, filling their ears with fear.

'The battle is on already – I've no time to explain. Unchain the one closest to the stairs. Hurry!'

After a moment of thought, Pale Face unchained the cannon and rattled it loose. He then nodded to the men who rushed to carry the heavy gun up the narrow stairs …

"Did it work?" the sailor asked as the old keeper paused to refill his tea. "The trick … the captain's idea … putting the cannon at the stern, did it work?" the sailor persisted.

The old keeper sighed. "No. The cannon was too heavy to handle. The men weren't trained for something like this. The ship was swinging, and they were shaky. They dropped it off the stern … the bloody fools dropped a cannon into the waters in the middle of battle." The old keeper took a mouthful of tea. "As the ship reached the fog, the captain drifted the ship sideways to face the pirates with fire. They were stationed in the middle of the fog, and everyone hoped that the pirates didn't follow them into it, but soon they saw the shadow of the pirates' ship coming toward them. The pirates were persistent and skilled. They angled their ship in a few seconds and hit first with double cannon lines on the starboard. They showered the captain's ship with fireballs, cracking wood, and bones."

"Sounds like you were there," the sailor said. "Were you?"

"No," he answered and gazed out of the window. "I wasn't, but a little boy was." …

… On the wooden floor of the main deck, a young boy curled his knees to his chest, covering both ears with his hands and shutting his eyes in fear. He could still hear everything, though, the footsteps around him, the screams of the wounded and the silence of the dead. Wood shattered and cracked with every cannonball that hit the ship. The sounds were deafening. Too loud to fade away, and he wanted them to stop, but the sounds – screams and booms – went on and on relentlessly.

He wished it would end and shut his eyes harder and pressed on his ears firmer. The longer the battle went on, the harder he wanted it to end. Until suddenly, it happened. The battle sounds stopped. Slowly he opened his eyes and cautiously uncovered his ears.

The cannons were silent, and a voice came from the high mast, shouting, 'It's the Merchant … It's the Merchant'.

Chapter 4

The sailor sat forward in his chair. "The Merchant?"

The old keeper held up his hand. "Let me continue." …

… 'It's the Merchant, the Merchant.' The boy heard one of the crew shout over and over.

Pale Face jumped onto the main deck, grabbed the boy from the floor, lifted him with his arm around his waist, and hurried to the stern facing the horizon.

'Look, boy, look.' Pale Face pointed the boy's attention away from all the blood and the dead.

It was hard to get a clear sea view in all the fog and cannon smoke. However, the Merchant's fleet was hard to miss no matter how thick the fog was. The boy glimpsed shadows of small ships approaching slowly as the pirates stood still, not attempting to board or fire at the captain's ship.

'They've stopped the fight,' the boy shouted. 'They're just watching us now.' He pointed towards the pirates, motionless on their vessel. 'How did this happen?'

'Because the Merchant is here, boy,' Pale Face said. 'In the Merchant's presence, the guns grow silent. The Merchant doesn't take sides. On the contrary, he helps the ones in need. He will not attack the pirates but will not leave us to them. Instead, the Merchant will tow us to a safe harbour, and if the pirates try to stop him or dare to fire one cannonball at one of his ships, he will blow them away in a heartbeat.'

One of the Merchant's ships ripped through the fog and smoke and gently bumped into the captain's ship. The ship had a small crew of five to seven men. The boy gazed at the ship. Somehow all the crew looked alike to him. They wore the same black trousers, boots and white cotton jackets with a wide black belt tied around their waists to keep the buttonless jackets closed. They seemed strong. Their shaved heads gave them a tough appearance, and their daring silent looks reinforced this.

'Are they brothers?' the boy asked Pale Face.

'Sort of. I bet you have never seen Asians before. They are from a far land where the sun rises.'

Small ships joined the other one – which looked identical to the first.

The boy watched on until the ship was engulfed by the smaller ones from all sides, filling the narrow gap between the captain's ship and the pirates.

The pirates remained motionless while the Merchant's fleet passed through.

Pale Face pointed towards the horizon as the sun's rays swept away the mist. 'The Merchant saved us. Look, the sun is out.'

The boy held up his palms and smiled. 'Yes, look, the sun is on my hands. Is that him? The Merchant?' He pointed at one of the larger ships that followed the smaller ones.

'No, that is not him,' Pale Face said, 'not in those.'

The boy waited as more ships passed until even larger vessels appeared. 'Then he must be in these.'

'Young fella, those are for the sailors.'

The boy pointed at an even larger ship. 'This must be his ship.'

Pale Face laughed. 'What are you thinking? That the Merchant would stay in one of those? Those ships are carrying his fleet's supplies. I told you it is the largest fleet on the ocean, and he has the biggest ship.'

'Bigger than that one?'

'Yes,' Pale Face said.

The boy turned and looked him in the eyes. 'Then how big

is his ship?' But before Pale Face could reply, shade swept slowly over the boy's face. He looked at his hands again and realised the sunlight was gone.

Pale Face smiled and pointed upwards. 'It is that big.'

The boy followed Pale Face's gaze. His jaw dropped open, and his eyes widened at the sight before him. He had never seen a ship so huge, a ship that blocked out the sun as everyone now stood in the shadow of the mighty vessel.

'That is Venus,' Pale Face said. 'The biggest ship in all seas. That is the Merchant's ship.'

Chapter 5

The sailor leant forward as if about to speak but then sat back and allowed the old keeper to carry on with the story.

"No one knew his name," the old keeper said, "but his reputation was well-known. It was common knowledge that he owned the largest fleet on all seas, larger than any kingdom's navy at that time. Armed stronger than any army, with longer-range cannons than any other vessel. Unbreakable swords with the sharpest blades, countless men and arms. Although he had that power and lived in an age of raids where power served greed, he never attacked, raided, or violated. He was a man of principles who kept his promises and fulfilled his word. He could have taken any kingdom or raided any city. But instead, he defended the weak and rescued the helpless. Though at that time, the seas were much more dangerous than they are nowadays, no pirate had ever dared to attack him. No one could face the Merchant's fire force. So, he sailed safely across the oceans with that fleet and became the biggest trader in the world. He reached lands beyond anyone's reach, bringing things no one had seen before, and traded with everyone, the poor, the rich and even royalty. He had a fortune of gold bigger than any man's greed, yet he was humble and kind. He provided the poor with provisions before offering them to the rich. Yet, no one knew his name. No one knew where he came from or where he was born. No one knew how he started his fleet or how it grew that big. His fleet was like a small floating village itself." The old keeper held his arms out wide. "A thousand ships! At that time, the biggest armadas were made up of 200, 300 or even 400 ships, but the Merchant had a thousand. It was the biggest fleet, and he owned the biggest ship of all, The Venus."

"Venus?" the sailor said. "Venus, as in the Roman goddess of beauty?"

"Yes," the old keeper said.

"Why was it named so? Was it beautiful?"

"The ship was made of dark reddish-brown wood, polished like new, that shone under the sun. Ledges, rails, doors and corridors were capped and decorated with real gold, with its name written in gold on the ship's sides. And the figurehead ..." The old keeper, wide-eyed, looked at the sailor. "At the bow was Venus herself, a figurehead made of pure gold. She looked magnificent as she glided over the waters. The ship was the most beautiful and the most powerful. Three times higher than the highest ship, five times wider than the broadest ship, and ninety cannons strong. But it wasn't just a ship. It was the Merchant's home. The Merchant built a house on its main deck, not a cabin, but a two-storey high house, and, because he loved the smell of freshly baked bread, the cook would bake it in front of his house every morning."

The sailor scoffed. "Bake? How did they bake fresh bread in ovens on a ship?"

"They had everything: food, fresh water. Some say they even grew their crops on the ships. They had cooks, tailors, carpenters and healers, everything one could ever need."

"It is hard to believe," the sailor said. "I mean, I've never seen anything close to what you are describing, especially that house thing on Venus, and I have sailed the seas for many years."

"It is all true. Venus was the wonder of all ships. Sailors' stories, at the time, were all about her. Not just because of its beauty but because it was rumoured the Merchant's gains were stored in the belly of the vessel throughout all his expeditions. Its lower deck was said to have had more gold than the richest kingdom, and it all belonged to one man, the Merchant."

"The captain's ship must have felt lucky to be rescued by the Merchant," the sailor said.

The old keeper smiled. "Yes, lucky indeed."

Then, the sailor asked, "So after he towed them, what happened next?"

"After they were safely away from the pirates, the Merchant's healers boarded the ship to treat the wounded using a special kind of medicine from the Orient."

The sailor nodded slowly. "Carry on with your story." The old keeper smiled …

… 'Why aren't they wearing any earrings?' the boy asked Pale Face. Apart from the Merchant's crew outfit and looks, the young boy couldn't help noticing that all the Merchant's crew were not wearing earrings. The young boy knew that sailors wore gold or silver earrings, so if they died or were helplessly ill, their mates could take them off to sell and pay for their journey back home.

'They don't wear earrings,' Pale Face answered.

'But why? How would they get home?'

Pale Face looked at the Merchant's men in respect and admiration and answered the boy, 'They will never need to because, to them, … the sea is their home.'

Chapter 6

The sailor cupped his hands around his mug. "I understand the seas were different from nowadays, but—"

"And the lands, too."

"How were they different?"

The old keeper began, "While the Merchant mastered the sea, kings ruled the lands. The Red Marbled Kingdom and the Silver Kingdom were the strongest, commonly known as the Silvers and the Reds. The two kingdoms shared a border and a history. The Reds had a long line of monarchs – strong, victorious kings who invaded one neighbouring kingdom after another – adding region after region until its lands were vast. The Silver Kingdom sat high on a hill surrounded by sea waters from three sides and shared a narrow land border downhill with the Reds. The Silvers felt cornered, so they were the first ally and hand shaker with the Reds."

The old keeper paused briefly, glancing at the sailor, before continuing, "Together, they invaded five of the seven regions that made up the world back then until one day, the Silver King died. His son rose to the throne but was against the alliance, invasion, war, and against submission. So, the Silvers refused to join forces with the Reds for the first time. To save his pride, the Red King waged war against the Silvers, attempting to wipe them out. But the outcome was unexpected.

Geography had the final say. The hill had a narrow entrance with sharp, rough rocks. The Red's powerful and large cavalry were not skilled enough to climb uphill and meet the Silvers' forces, so they were stationed at the foot. Foolishly, the Silvers rushed downhill to meet the Reds. Meanwhile, at sea, the Reds' warships sailed out of the Crab Gulf that the Red Kingdom overlooked. The gulf was enclosed by two mainland formations resembling crab's arms, hence the name. On the east side, the hill stretched into the sea. And on the other side, the west, several isles, an archipelago, formed close to the structure of crab claws. These isles were green, full of trees, and called the Tear Drop Isles. The Silvers' navy – three-hundred ships and highly-skilled sailors – waited for the Red's vessels outside the Crab Gulf and instantly engulfed them when they appeared. The Reds were defeated, wiped out, and sent to the seabed by the mighty Silver armada. The Reds won on land but couldn't pursue and wipe out the Silvers uphill. The Silvers won at sea, but their cannons couldn't reach the Red Marbled Castle and destroy it. So, the two kingdoms stayed in this endless standoff. For years, neither one could attack nor drawback. And the Merchant was a friend to both."

Chapter 7

The sailor shifted in his seat but said nothing. He glanced outside at the ominous sky and then nodded for the old keeper to continue …

… 'What's that?' the boy said, looking wide-eyed at Pale Face as a second cannon boomed loudly and echoed from afar.

'Don't worry,' Pale Face said and pointed across the bay. 'It is the Silver fleet announcing the Merchant's arrival and welcoming him into their harbour. They are firing their cannons to honour and welcome him.'

"Every kingdom welcomed the Merchant," the old keeper said. "His arrival was festive to everyone, especially the poor, who rushed to shore with smiles. To them, the Merchant's arrival meant salvation. The Merchant's first day of arrival was called the *No Trade Day*, where trading was forbidden. He dedicated the day to those who were in need. First, he gave away gold and silver coins to the poor, clothes to the needy and then spent the rest of the day treating and healing the weak and ill. His arrival in any kingdom was widely celebrated. People admired his kindness, were in awe of his superiority and were fascinated and intrigued with the Merchant."

"Tell me more," the sailor said …

… Pale Face grabbed the young boy's hand as they blended into the festive crowd ashore. At the same time, a mysterious veiled man stood in the group, his eyes locked on the ship that the Merchant had rescued from the pirates. He remained silent, unlike the rest of the cheering crowd.

It was a custom that the royal guards received the Merchant at the castle's gate. They lined up in two rows opposite each other, creating a corridor of guards for the Merchant to walk down.

After passing the silver sea gate, the Merchant anchored his fleet in the middle of Crab Gulf – in front of the Red Kingdom's castle. Unfortunately, no dockland was big enough to host his enormous armada, so a small boat travelled across the shallow waters. It ferried the Merchant onto the land, the ceremonial guards lined up, stretching from shore to the Red Castle's gate. His fleet would pass through the silver sea gate, allowing entry into the Crab Gulf, and then the Merchant would travel through the Red Kingdom until finally ascending the hill to the Silver Kingdom.

The Merchant stomped the shore with his foot. The guards announced his arrival by calling loudly and repeatedly, 'The Merchant … it's the Merchant'. Red guards at the gate echoed back, as did the guards inside the castle. The noise was tremendous as 'the Merchant, the Merchant' echoed across the land.

The Merchant walked through the red-marbled floored hallways of the Red Castle.

Daylight beamed through tiny windows that barely had any view. The castle's front had many windows, but many were decoys. These fake windows had been made to deceive the Silvers if they attacked the castle with arrows or cannonballs. Confusing the Silvers so they were unsure where in the castle the King's Hall, dining hall, or the Queen's chamber lay …

The old keeper suddenly paused, deep in thought, rubbing at his bristled chin.

"I am listening," the sailor said, but the old keeper remained deep in thought. "Hello?" the sailor said louder.

"Oh, sorry … what was I saying?" the old keeper said,

refixing his attention back to the sailor.

"The decoy windows …" the sailor prompted him. "The Red Kingdom, the King's Hall, the Queen's chamber."

"Oh … Yes, of course," the old keeper said, then paused again.

"Are you alright?"

"Me? Yes … I'm fine."

The sailor narrowed his eyes. "You don't seem fine to me. What's wrong?"

"I just remembered …" the old keeper mumbled.

"What did you remember, old mate?"

"I remembered … She."

"She?" the sailor said. "Her, you mean. You remembered her."

"The Queen. I remembered the Queen."

Chapter 8

The old keeper sighed. "Long ago, kings and princes fought for land and wealth. They wanted more and more, never stopping in this quest. It was an hour-by-hour battle in which the winner took it all. No king could satisfy their desire for wealth, power, land, castles, and armies. Yet, amid all that greed, no king craved anything more than winning the Queen's heart. To be with the Queen was a dream, a desire, a challenge. She was beauty in human form."

"How beautiful was she?" the sailor asked. "What did she look like?"

The old keeper smiled. "It wasn't only about how she looked but how she was. She was the Queen by birth and had never been called by her Christian name. She had always been addressed as the Queen since she was a little girl. She was spoiled and obeyed. She moved about barefoot, any place, whatever time it was, morning or night. They wiped the marble floors until they gleamed like a mirror just for her. And she loved to dance. Whenever she signalled, music played, and she danced, oh did she dance. She moved to music better than a silk curtain to a summer breeze. She wasn't the most beautiful in the land, but she owned her beauty. She had the fairest snow-white skin and bathed in cream and rose petals that her virgin servants picked for her every morning. She wasn't the most beautiful but had the longest, thickest, and straightest hair. Her servants combed her hair a thousand times every night. She wasn't the most beautiful but had the most expressive eyes that magnified her emotions in an unforgettable look. On the night she was born, her family was murdered in an attempted coup. It was foiled by her guardian – a master guard of unmatched skills and strength. He looked after her as she grew up dancing barefoot in the halls of her royal palace. Every king and prince, far and wide, wanted to win her hand, but she could never be won. Even the best of them got nothing more than her contempt." The old keeper smiled again. "She wasn't the most beautiful. No, she wasn't, but she was pride and glamour, and she was *the Queen*. When she turned eighteen, her kingdom grew weak with political turmoil, and her army fell apart. It was only a matter of time until a stronger empire invaded her lands and threw the Queen and her people into slavery. The Queen then used her sharpest and most important weapon – her mind. She announced that her hand would be given in marriage and spread the word to every royal court. Kings went crazy, for they deeply desired the Queen. So she invited them to the palace, to a Ceremonial Royale pageant, a proposal, and a wedding at the same time. Kings arrived from around the world and found the Queen, in her wedding dress, sitting on her throne, awaiting her dream man. The successful royal suitor, a prince, or a king would be chosen by her. One by one, they all stepped in front of her and kissed her hand. It was announced that the one she accepted was to hold her hand and walk her through the hall. The rest would instantly be considered mere invitees, witnesses – envious witnesses – to the regal event." The old keeper coughed and cleared his throat.

"Of course, all the suitors brought wonderful presents to impress the Queen, and she received a pile of valuables higher than all of her kingdom's debts. The presents could have saved her kingdom, but she knew wealth alone wasn't enough. Power must be added to the equation. She needed to stand in the shadow of a strong king – a king of kings, someone who would be feared and admired across the globe. With the might of her beauty, she had the chance to choose any king. But, unbeknown to the royal court, guests and dignitaries – and before anyone had stepped foot into the hall of the Ceremonial Royale – she had already picked her king. The strongest and wealthiest. The Red King."

Chapter 9

The old keeper clasped his hands together. "Let me tell you about the Ceremonial Royale."

"The what?" the sailor said.

"All will become clear," the old keeper said. "The Red King, although the wealthiest, knew the competition was fierce, and wealth alone would not be enough to impress the Queen. The assembled guests at the Ceremonial Royale expected the Red King to walk through the reception with tons of gems and gold, for his wealth was legendary. However, to the astonishment of everyone, the Red King walked down the aisle towards the Queen – who sat gracefully on her throne in her wedding dress – with nothing. No treasure chests full of gold. No crowns or tiaras. No exotic animals from faraway lands. Nothing. Only his royal guards and himself. He knew he had already captured the Queen's attention and approached the Queen with nothing but a smile. But as he reached her, he pulled aside his cape and held out the Queen's gift he had concealed. She gasped. It was unlike anything she had ever seen. In fact, no one had ever seen. In his hands, the Red King held a pair of crystal shoes decorated with diamonds and rubies, which sparkled like stars. The Queen was speechless, enrapt and dazzled by their beauty." The old keeper held up his hands as if displaying the shoes and continued, "The Red King bent down on one knee, kissed her hand, and deftly slipped the shoes onto the Queen's feet. The Red King was clever. He knew the Queen would never be won by the most expensive gift but rather by the one-of-a-kind. Something unique. He kissed her hand again, took it in his, stood and walked hand in hand with her down the aisle. The other envious suitors could do nothing but clap and cheer as the Red King married the Queen …"

The Queen was in her royal chamber when the voices of the guards echoed through the halls with news of the Merchant's arrival.

Her maids – dressed in white silk, long-haired and fair – who always accompanied her within her chamber rushed to dress and ready her. The guards she had brought from her home kingdom – resplendent in gold and gleaming armour – waited to escort her to him.

The Queen – in a dazzlingly beautiful dress flowing majestically behind her – waited for a guard to open the door, then glided, almost floating, through as she hurried barefoot to welcome the Merchant.

The Merchant entered the royal hall, the red hall, where the King sat on his throne.

'Greetings, your Highness,' the Merchant said as he stood in front of the Red King.

'Welcome, my friend,' the Red King said. 'It's been a long while.'

'Yes, your Highness, we have stretched our sail beyond seas and rocks.'

The Red King smiled. 'How far did you sail this time? You must tell me all about it.'

'I have sailed far enough to bring you these, your Grace.' The Merchant waved his men forward, who promptly presented several chests.

It was a tradition that the Merchant gave exotic gifts to kings and queens upon his arrival in their lands. Gifts like silk, spices and even gems.

'More gifts?' The King smiled again. 'Every time you arrive?'

'It is the least I can do, your Highness,' the Merchant answered.

At that moment, the Queen entered the hall.

The Red King waved his wife closer. 'Come, my queen, see our friend's surprising gift.'

The Queen glanced first at the Merchant and then the chests before she looked at the Merchant again. 'You are always most welcome here,' she said without smiling.

The Merchant nodded at her as she sat next to her husband.

The Merchant's gifts were extraordinary, exceptional pieces from every land. The Red King and the Queen were delighted, opening one chest after another until the last one, an iron chest with little holes, remained.

The Merchant's men carried it forward and placed it in front of the Red King and his queen. But, unlike all the previous chests, the Merchant's men didn't open this one themselves. Instead, they stepped back and allowed the Merchant to move forward. He laid his hand on the iron box and looked at the King. 'Your Highness, this is my special gift to you.'

The King was eager to see the Merchant's unique gift. Of course, all the Merchant's gifts were exceptional and exotic, but when the Merchant himself called a present 'special', it must be something extraordinary.

The Merchant opened the iron chest – it was more of a cage, to be precise – then carefully dipped his arms, elbows deep, inside and slowly removed a newly born animal.

'What is that?' the Queen asked. 'Is it sleeping?' She narrowed her eyes. 'It looks like a newly born bear, maybe?'

'No,' the Red King said, 'it is more of a wolf or a dog, its fur … or is that horsehair?' They stared at the Merchant.

'This is a rare animal, your Highness,' he said. 'The tribe that gave it to me calls it, in their native language, the Beast.' The Merchant then pulled a second from the iron box. 'I have brought you, twins of the Beast, your Highness. Their mother was slain by ruthless hunters who killed it because of a belief that it produces a magical secretion through its fur as soon as it gives birth. I tried to save her, but it was too late. In gratitude, the tribe gave me the twins, and now I present them to your Grace as a humble gift. Cage them behind walls, your Highness. Feed them through iron bars until they grow strong, and when they do, nothing will protect you better than these Beasts.'

The Red King and the Queen looked at each other and grinned. Then the Red King broke the silence. 'Your present is warmly accepted,' he said, then ordered his guards to take the animals to the dungeons.

'Thank you,' the Queen said.

The Merchant smiled and nodded. 'Your Grace.'

Chapter 10

The window slammed open as the winds battered the seashore. The old keeper slowly got to his feet, closed it, wandered across to the stove, and stirred the pot of stew. It was half-cooked.

"That smells delicious," the sailor commented.

The old keeper returned to his seat and eased himself back into the chair.

"When did this happen?" the sailor asked.

The old keeper scratched his bristled chin. "Does it matter?"

"Not really ..." The sailor shrugged. "Yes, maybe it does. I can't believe someone could get that powerful nowadays. I mean ... like the Merchant. Or even a couple of decades ago. The world is getting harder and harder. For instance, if I wanted to be like him, it would be impossible."

The old keeper looked the sailor in the eyes, took a deep breath, and continued the story ...

... The Queen's maids lived in the castle, in one chamber. Movement around the court was rigorous, and their movement in and out of the castle was prohibited. Except for one. Her first maid.

The Red King had only one trusted minister since he inherited the throne, expanded his kingdom, and built his empire. Though close to the Red King himself, the Minister rarely asked the Red King for anything. The Red King admired that about him. The Minister had only asked for a favour when his daughter turned into a beautiful young woman. The Minister had asked the King to appoint her as the Queen's first maid. The Red King, of course, welcomed the Minister's request. And so, she became the Queen's first maid – the only one with the privilege of taking one day off every week. She slept over at her father's humble house. Her father had never wanted to live in the castle, though the Red King offered him a room. The Minister had declined, insisting he preferred to stay in the same cottage he had lived in with his late wife. He had told the Red King it was a way to cherish his memories. It was another thing the Red King admired about his minister.

But that never made his daughter happy. A single sleepover in her father's house every week, limited movement in and out and even around the Red Castle was frustrating. Being the Queen's first maid, or even just one of her maids, wasn't just a full-time occupation. It was her life. Her whole life. Dedicated to the Queen's service. She wanted a life of her own. She wanted a life for herself.

The Red King and the Queen receiving the Merchant was one of the few opportunities the maids had to do whatever they felt like – resting, napping, giggling, reading or even taking a brief stroll through the royal gardens. Each maid did something different, and the first maid always did the same thing. She ran to the same place to see the same person, her only love, the Merchant's First Man.

'I have missed you,' the First Man said as he hugged the first maid, or Prima as the Queen called her.

'Longing for you is torture,' Prima said. 'I can't express my feeling of despair when you left.' She pulled away from his hug to gaze at his face. 'And the worst thing is I never know when you are coming back.'

'I am back now, aren't I?' he said to Prima and placed his hand on her cheek. 'Look what I've got you.' He opened a small wooden box with a diamond ring inside it. 'This is a diamond, Prima. It is said to have been originally coal, but somehow, it turns into a diamond after being deeply embraced by mighty mountains. Your love embraced my heart, turning every piece of black coal in my world into a sparkling diamond.'

The pair, locked in an embrace, spoke softly, whispering to each other at the far end of the royal gardens. The First Man knew how to sneak in without being spotted by the castle's guards.

A bell rang. Prima turned sharply to where the sound came from. It came from the castle. 'Oh no. That soon?' she said and groaned. The bell ringing was the Queen's call for her maids to be back – an ornate, crystal bell with a golden handle that she rang rapidly.

The lovers stepped away from each other while still holding hands. 'When will I see you again?' she asked.

He kissed her hand. 'After tomorrow, my love.'

The bell rang faster and faster, indicating the Queen's impatience.

'I have to run back to the castle,' she said as they stretched their arms long enough to let go of each other's hands.

He stepped back into the bushes and paused at the foot of a tree. 'After tomorrow, my love. After Market Day.'

Chapter 11

Down the dark streets of the Red Kingdom, the Red King's Minister, wearing a veil, walked through the village until he reached the bar and entered. The bar was full of chattering, laughing, eating, and drinking customers. The Minister, ignoring the crowd, stealthily made his way to the far end and sat at a table hidden behind a pillar.

The bartender, who had seen him enter, walked across to him and lowered his head. 'A Black Collar is here,' he whispered. The Minister grimaced, got to his feet and followed him to a wooden door behind the bar. The bartender held it open and allowed the Minister to step into the dimly lit stairway and make his way down to a room below. In the middle of the room was a table and two chairs, one occupied by a man dressed in black.

'It has been a while since you have been here in person,' the Minister said as he removed his veil and sat in front of the Black Collar.

'It has,' the Black Collar said. 'The Dean is wondering how much longer you need to take to find a solution to our problem?' He sneered. 'The Merchant, in case you need me to remind you.'

The Minister shuffled on his seat. 'Soon.'

The Black Collar banged his fist down on the table. 'Soon! Do you want me to convey your idiotic answer to the Dean? Soon is what you said long ago, and what have you done since? What have you even planned?'

The Minister remained silent as the Black Collar sneered again. 'You are nothing but a stupid bastard, aren't you, Minister?'

The minister jumped to his feet. 'Enough with your rudeness.'

'Enough with your procrastination,' the Black Collar shouted as he stood. 'You are playing and wasting the family's time and resources. Do you think that you can play the Blacks?'

The Minister slumped back onto his chair. 'It is a matter of timing,' he said, mopping the beads of sweat from his forehead. 'It will happen soon.'

The Black Collar slowly walked around the table and growled, pushing his face closer to the Minister's. 'Timing,' he said. 'What is important, and the only thing that matters now, is the family's business – the Black family's trade which the Merchant is destroying.' He stood upright again and proceeded to slowly circle the Minister. 'We are down to one-tenth of what we used to make, and the Dean is fed up.' The Black Collar pointed his finger at the Minister. 'Find a solution or be one,' he said, snatching up his coat. 'And make it soon.' He walked towards the door and glared at the Minister.

'What is that supposed to mean?' the Minister said, frowning deeply.

'You'll find out. But for now, no payments until you figure out a plan and take action.'

Chapter 12

After a long day of helping people, the Merchant returned to his ship to dress up for the Red King's dinner. He would rather have skipped it but couldn't turn down the Red King's invitation.

Music played, and food of all colours and tastes was set on a long wooden oak table. Dancers swirled around. The Merchant finished his meal first, although he had eaten nowhere near as much as the Red King. The Queen, however, barely ate anything, spending most of the meal pushing her food around her plate.

The Red King patted his stomach. 'Well, that is what I call a king-size meal.' He banged the table with his fists, and a servant rushed to refill the King's cup. He snatched up his drink and stood. 'Merchant,' he said, 'would you join me on the terrace? That fat turkey I ate pushed out all the air in my chest. I need a fresh breeze.'

The Merchant stood. 'Of course, your Highness.'

The pair wandered outside as the Queen silently listened to the music play.

The terrace was vast, overlooking the woods at the back of the castle.

'Ah, air, fresh air. I love this terrace. Too bad it is not facing the sea.' He growled. 'If it weren't for those bloody Silvers, my terrace would be overlooking it.' He staggered and grabbed hold of the stone balustrade that ran around the terrace. 'I would have had any terrace in the world,' he slurred.

The Merchant joined the King. 'Make peace with them, and you won't have to hide your open spaces or narrow your windows.'

'What?' the Red King said and turned to the Merchant. 'Peace? With them?' The Red King sneered. 'They want no peace. I have tried to make a deal a thousand times. Yet…' He swept his hand out in front of him. 'None.'

'They didn't refuse peace,' the Merchant said. 'They refused war, your Highness. If your deal requires them to help you invade the rest of the world, then, yes, there will never be peace.'

'What are you asking me to do? Huh? You said it yourself, the rest of the world. I am almost the King of the world.' He turned and pointed upwards. 'Look at those. Seven poles but only five flags, seven poles for the seven corners of the world. My grandfather put one flag up there. My father also, but I …' He patted his chest. 'I added three flags, three!' The King thrust three fingers in the air. 'They spent their lifetimes adding one, and I added three corners of the world to the Red Kingdom.' He scowled. 'But these three mean nothing to me unless I have the other two. Then I will truly be the King of the world. Not an almost King of the world.'

The Merchant followed the King back inside as the tempo of the music changed. Then, as the musicians increased the volume, the servants busied themselves with emptying the hall of tables and chairs. The Queen, who had removed her shoes, and now stood barefoot on the red marble floor, started to dance.

The Red King smiled and gazed at his wife as the Merchant and everyone else watched. The crowd gasped as she danced. Captivated by her elegance and poise.

She danced and danced, and as her dance neared its end, the Merchant asked the Red King's pardon and left the hall. The Queen stopped dancing as she saw the Merchant leave. She paused, breathed deeply, and watched him walk out.

Chapter 13

It was the Merchant's Market Day, and people in nearby villages rushed to the Red Kingdom's marketplace. They arrived in huge numbers early in the morning – the rich, the moderate, the humble and the servants. Everyone wanted to attend the Merchant's Market Day.

His men had set up extra tents – to accommodate the multitude of visitors – which stretched out along the length of the marketplace. There was something of interest for everyone.

The Merchant never attended the market but supervised the merchandise taken from his ships and waited by the docks to personally check the unsold pieces before they were put back into storage.

He delegated the market's trades to his First Man, which made it the busiest day for his subordinate. Although tiring, the First Man was always up to the job, always reliable and trustworthy. The Merchant trusted him implicitly. The list of items brought from the ship was enormous. Clothes, spices, ornaments, crystals, gems, jewellery, exotic animals, and herbs from every part of the globe were for sale.

The veiled man from the bar strolled around the market, examining the items for sale, observing every detail and making a mental note of the tents and trades present. Especially the number of Merchant's guards who had been sent to secure the market.

The veiled man continued to roam around the marketplace.

When satisfied and before he caught the attention of the Merchant's guards, he jumped on his horse and swiftly rode away. He sped on through the woods until in sight of the Red Castle, where he stopped, dismounted, took off his veil and cape, and secreted them inside a bag hanging from the saddle. Then, remounting, he rode onwards towards the Red Castle as fast as his horse would take him. The guards, who saw him riding towards them, quickly sprang into action. 'The Minister, it's the King's Minister. Open the gate immediately,' they shouted atop the walls. The gate swung open as the Minister reached the threshold, and the guards saluted him as the horse and rider galloped by.

The Minister hurried to the throne hall, ignoring the saluting royal guards, and marched up to the Red King. 'Your royal Highness,' the Minister said as he bowed.

'I haven't seen you since yesterday,' the Red King said. 'You weren't even here for the Merchant's reception.'

'I would rather watch your back, Sire. I was gathering intelligence.'

'As usual.'

'I am at your service, your Highness.' the Minister said and quickly bowed again.

The Red King plucked a grape from a bunch next to his throne, and, popping it into his mouth, he appraised his Minister. 'And what did you find out this time?'

'He saved another ship.'

The Red King waved a dismissive hand. 'I don't know why this worries you so much.'

The Minister steeled himself. 'Sire, it means one thing, and it is the only thing that should concern your kingdom. His fleet is getting bigger and more powerful than any other, and no pirate can defeat him. No pirate dare attack him. He is the strongest out there on the seas. The seas are our weakness. Your Highness, you see him as a friend, but I see him as a threat, especially because he is not just a friend of yours. He is friends with everyone, even the Silvers, our arch enemy.' The Minister lowered his head and kept his eyes on the ground as he finished.

The Red King took a deep breath and exhaled as he looked across at the narrow windows of his hall that barely let light in.

'All that stands between you and the world is a strong fleet,' The Minister continued. 'And the Merchant has the biggest one. The Red crown could rule the world for a thousand years if only you could get the Merchant to join us. He may agree one day, but until that day comes, the Merchant, your friend, is a threat to your realm, Sire.'

The Red King remained silent, looking at the Minister standing before him. 'You may go,' he said. 'Go now.' The King waved his hand and turned away from the Minister.

The Minister sighed. 'Yes, Sire.' He nodded, bowed and strode out of the throne hall.

Chapter 14

Luckily, Prima's day off followed Market Day, and the First Man was free, so they spent the whole day together. A picnic date was their favourite, by a lake, in a hidden spot wrapped around by trees, plants and flowers. The light breeze, sun rays and birds singing made the day even more perfect. They loved being there, and they loved being with each other.

Prima smiled and lay her head on the First Man's lap. 'So, you have seen the whole world?' she said.

'Yes, I have,' he answered while tenderly running his fingers through her hair.

She sat up. 'Then tell me how it feels.' Her eyes widened. 'How does it feel to step into a new town and meet new people with completely different cultures? What is that like?'

He lifted his hand and placed it on her cheek. 'When you arrive in a town you have never been to, you must feel it before exploring it.' he said. 'You must fill your senses with it. You see it with your eyes, you feel it with your hands by touching its walls and houses, you taste it by eating its food, and you hear it by listing to its music. You inhale it by taking a deep breath over its highest hill. Only then do you get to truly feel it.'

Prima frowned. 'You make it sound like a person.'

'Well, towns are made of people. People are towns. I've always felt that women are like towns.'

'So, I am a town.' Prima smiled. 'So how do you feel me?

I don't have streets or houses or music bands.'

'I see you by looking at every inch of you and every detail of your beauty. I go to your favourite places, listen to your favourite music, taste your favourite food, inhale the scents of your favourite flowers. Everything I see, touch, smell or taste makes me fall in love with you more and more.'

She giggled. 'So, what would you call me if I were a town?'

'You?' He rubbed his chin.

'Yes.' Prima shook him gently.

His eyes filled with tears. 'Home. You are home, Prima. You are my home.'

Chapter 15

The Red King strolled through the royal garden with the Queen as her maids and his guards followed a step behind. The Red King smiled, and the Queen, although slightly preoccupied, still listened as he spoke.

The guards behind them stomped their spears and announced, 'The Merchant.'

The Red King and Queen turned to find the Merchant striding towards them.

'Your royal Highness, your Majesty,' he greeted the Red King and the Queen.

'Perfect timing,' the Red King said. 'We were just about to ride out.' He pointed to two horses in front of the royal stables. 'Join us. I will have my Arabian horse ready in a blink.'

'I appreciate it, but no need, your Highness,' the Merchant said. 'I came to bid you farewell. Tomorrow is No Land Day. My crew and I stay aboard the whole day and prepare for the next sail. No one is allowed to step onto land, and we will be sailing out the day after.'

'Oh, yes,' the Red King said and mounted his horse. 'No Land Day already? I thought you would be spending more days here. Well, we will see you next time. Try to come back soon.' The Red King looked at the Queen, who hadn't mounted her horse. 'Aren't you joining me, my Queen?'

'No,' she said. 'I will be heading back to my chamber, for my mind had slipped a matter I need to attend to.'

'Very well.' The Red King frowned, then turned to the Merchant. 'Are you sure you don't want to join me now, Merchant? There is a free horse right here.' He pointed to the Queen's horse.

No one is ever allowed to ride the King's or the Queen's horses, the Merchant thought and answered, 'Thank you, your Grace, but as a matter of fact, I don't ride horses.'

The King laughed. 'You don't ride?'

'I ride waves, your Highness. Only waves.'

'Right.' The Red King smiled, then said, 'Well then, have a safe ride.' He nodded at the Merchant, glanced at his wife and rode off as mounted royal guards followed.

As the Red King and his guards reached the wooded tree line and disappeared from sight, the Queen turned sharply to face the Merchant. 'What are you doing?' she whispered.

'I am not doing anything,' he said.

'Exactly.' She gazed at him. 'You are not doing anything. You are not answering my letters. You do not love me back.'

The Merchant thrust his arms behind his back. 'I have never read the letters you sent me. Therefore, how could I answer?'

The Queen lowered her eyes. 'Why are you doing this?'

The Merchant glanced in the direction the King had gone. 'You shouldn't be writing to me. You are a married woman, and I would never stab any man in his back.'

'But…' She stepped closer to him. 'Please read them. Please read my letters. I want you to know how I feel. I—'

'I know how you feel, and you must stop,' the Merchant said.

'Stop!' The Queen glowered at him. 'You are telling me to stop? I am not the one who should be stopping anything. You are the one who should stop.'

The Merchant rolled his eyes. 'Me? Stop what? I have nothing to—'

'Stop this.' She waved her hand out in front of her. 'All this. The fleet, the Merchant, master of the seas, a friend of kings and queens, the man who owns Venus – the ship with a golden belly. Stop all those stories about you, the admiration and the wonder.

Stop this magical world of yours, where you have no equal. Stop being this noble savage who is feared and loved at the same time. Stop being like no other, stop being the Merchant, stop being you … then I will stop.' She briefly stared at him as her top lip quivered, then turned quickly and hurried away as the Merchant stood in the royal gardens and watched her leave.

Chapter 16

The Minister woke early in the morning, put on his formal clothes and stepped downstairs. Prima sat at the wooden table in the humble dining room.

'Prima?' he said, 'shouldn't you be with the Queen at the Red Castle by now?'

'I'll be a little late, but it's all right,' she said, 'I've asked her permission.'

The Minister poured himself a cup of tea, sat at the head of the table and studied his daughter. 'Are you all right, my dear?'

'Yes, Father, don't worry.' She lowered her head a little. 'I … I just wanted to talk to you about a matter.'

He put his tea aside and leant in closer. 'What is it?' He smiled at her. 'You know you can tell me anything.'

Prima looked up at him. 'Someone asked for my hand in marriage.'

Her father raised his eyebrows. 'You've never failed to surprise me.'

'I love him, Father,' she said.

'Who is he?'

'The First Man,' Prima said quietly.

He frowned. 'Whose first man?'

'The First Man, Father.' Her eyes widened. 'The Merchant's First Man.'

'I want to spare you my mockery, but no matter what title they gave him on that ship, it is worthless here in this kingdom.'

He scoffed. 'The first man of a ship is a first of none. He is just a sailor, Prima.' He laughed and shook his head. 'You want to marry a sailor?'

Prima pouted at her father. 'A sailor is what he does, but it is not who he is.'

He stood and glared at his daughter. 'But that's what you will be, a sailor's wife, living on the crumbs of what the rich …' He turned with his hands behind his back and looked into the fireplace. 'You'll be left waiting for him on land while he leaves without knowing when you will see him again. You will be poor and worried. That's what you are asking my permission for?' He turned to face her again. 'You are the Royal Minister's daughter, my only daughter. You should marry a wealthy nobleman.' He slapped the table. 'Perhaps a prince or even a king one day.'

'But, Father—'

'No.' He turned away from her again. 'My answer is no.'

Prima placed her head on the table and sobbed.

The Minister took a deep breath and turned around. 'Prima,' he said, moving closer to her. 'Your mother and I have done everything, and I mean everything, to give you a happy and wealthy life. It's all been planned, and we have committed to the plan. I am not giving up now after all this.' He briefly closed his eyes. 'After your mother died, I promised … I promised on her death bed that I would make sure you married someone worthy.'

She dabbed at her eyes with a handkerchief. 'Maybe you won't be breaking your promise, but you will be breaking my heart.'

He growled. 'I swore to secure you. …' He thumped the table again. 'Why do you think I secured you a position in the castle in the first place? You are the Minister's daughter and the Queen's first maid. If you are going to step out of the castle, you should be stepping into another.' He turned sharply again and put his hands behind his back. 'I would only marry you into a wealthy and honourable marriage. Not a sailor.' He strode towards the door and paused at the threshold. 'I will see you at the castle, and don't be late.'

Prima put her head on the table and sobbed louder as she heard the door slam behind him.

Chapter 17

The Queen watched her maids fill her bathtub with creamy white water. Every night she bathed. The tub had been constructed in her chamber – carved into the marbled floor. Four wooden pillars hung with delicate white curtains on all four sides. Although gossamer-thin and see-through, they still gave the Queen a sense of royal exclusivity when closed. She not only liked that but also the way the curtains moved with the slightest breeze.

After filling the tub, the maids waited for her. Deep in thought, she stood and strolled across the chamber towards the tub. She handed her gown to one of the maids on the way, stepped lightly up to the marble platform and glided into the creamy water so smoothly that she hardly agitated the liquid. She bathed before sitting and shutting her eyes.

When finished, she stepped from the water, and her maids wrapped a purple silk robe around her. As was her custom, she sat at her dresser as Prima combed her hair. She had to comb the Queen's long hair every night in a thousand slow strokes while the maids stood around in service. The Queen stayed silent – deep in thought as Prima carried on the nightly duty.

That night, after the Queen had finished her beauty routine, she dismissed Prima and the other maids. They left and headed to their sleeping quarters adjacent to her Majesty's chamber. She stood by the dresser and, carrying a lamp, made her way to the narrow window next to her bed. She placed the lamp on the edge of the window, looked at the shadows of the Merchant's ships in the bay, and thought, Fine. Don't read my letters, but when you look at the castle, you will see my candle lit all night, and I know that you will know it's me. You will know that I am sleepless. You will know that between love and anger, I lay, restless, because of you.

The Queen wasn't the only one sleepless and restless that night.

Prima walked through the dark hallways in her nightgown. How could she sleep? The only one she had ever loved was about to sail off, and she didn't know when he would return. She reached the castle's top floor, and the Red guards let her pass – they were used to seeing her wander the halls at night. Tonight, as she took the stairs to the roof, it was with a heavy heart.

She stood under the moonlight and looked at the sea where the Merchant's fleet floated. The ships' lights sparkled over the waters – a thousand ships or more.

'I am sorry I had to tell you the harsh words my father told me. I am sorry you had to hear those things. I am sorry I can't comfort you now. I don't even know where you are. Where are you, my love? Which of those ships beholds you?' she whispered. 'I want to be with you. We belong together.' Tears dropped down her cheeks one after another.

Chapter 18

One of the Queen's guards made his way back to the castle and said to himself, 'What am I doing?' He had just delivered the Queen's sealed letter to the Merchant's fleet. He questioned it every time. 'Why does it have to be me? She orders me every time. Sneak out, go unnoticed to the Teardrop Isles, swim quietly to the Merchant's fleet, hand them the letter and sneak back in. Why doesn't she want anyone to know about it? What is in that letter? In all those letters? What if I get caught? Does the Red King know about this? Maybe she is doing it for him … some secret arrangement he has with the Merchant.' Finding comfort in the thought, he indulged in it and said, 'Well, that makes perfect sense, especially since the Silvers have their spies everywhere.' As he was about to rest on the thought, he remembered the Merchant had returned many letters without opening them. He was confused. This was too much for him to grasp and too threatening to linger around. He had to ask someone, but whom? The Queen? Of course not. The Red King, the Minister, no, no, no. Someone from the Red Castle, someone close to the Royals. 'Prima!' he shouted. 'I will ask Prima, and she will explain it to me. Or if she finds anything wrong with it, she will be the one to handle it. She will know what to do. She will. She must.'

As he approached the last isle facing the Red Castle, he stopped, looked around, ducked down and crept towards the shore. Then, spotting Red guards patrolling on the other side and realising he had to find Prima immediately, he dipped into the waters quietly and swam back to the Red Castle.

52

Chapter 19

After months at sea, the Merchant's fleet finally reached land. A faraway land out of the reach of the Red King. The furthest land of all, the kingdom of World's Edge, one of the few kingdoms behind rivers and seas that the Red King couldn't invade. World's Edge was a humble kingdom with the smallest castle, ruled by the oldest king.

As soon as the ships neared land, the Merchant took a small boat himself and landed. He was eager to reach the shore and didn't wait for his fleet to anchor.

The First Man knew the reason behind the Merchant's eagerness. Everyone knew. The Merchant jumped off the boat. With splashing steps, he made his way towards the shore. When he reached the beach, he ran and ran. His eagerness to see her was overwhelming. He ran to Isabella. Everyone knew her. Everyone knew her story.

Isabella's father was a gypsy, a traveller who met Isabella's mother one day in the woods near her camp. Her mother was from another clan, a Romanichal Traveller. Isabella's father fell in love with her exotic beauty as soon as he laid his eyes on her. She, too, fell in love with him.

They decided to get married, but she was promised to one of her cousins. Nonetheless, her stubbornness was greater than her clan's fury. After leaving her own clan and joining his, they married. She would have been happy, but they cursed her. Yes, her clan cursed her by the wolves – three fierce wolves.

She heard them howl every night, no matter where she travelled. She listened to the howling night after night, week after week, month after month. The wolves howled and followed. Isabella's parents tried to ignore the threat and live happily in love. They did for a while, but when she became pregnant, the howling got closer and louder, and fear grew and overshadowed their love and happiness. One moonless night she broke down. She was getting close to giving birth and feared for the lives of her beloved and child. She cried for hours. Angry to see her like that and fed up with the threat, Isabella's father took his axe and looked for the wolves. She couldn't stop him. No one could. Ignoring everyone's protestations, he marched into the dark woods. The people listened to the roars and screams until the sounds faded. He never returned. They searched for him and found one dead wolf he had managed to kill with his axe, but there was no sign of him.

Isabella was born a few days later. Grief drove everyone to resent her mother, and she felt unwanted by all. She could see it in their eyes and silent, gloomy faces. She knew it was only a matter of time before their gloom turned into anger, and anger washed away their patience.

Days passed, lonely and silent, until, after a whole year, on a moonless night, the wolves returned. Late at night, she heard them howl, and the howling got closer and closer. Taking baby Isabella to bed in her arms, she locked herself inside her wagon – a knife held tightly in her shaking hand – and waited.

The howling stopped, but then she heard twigs cracking outside her door. They were here, and she didn't know what to do other than stay still and quiet. Her wagon was parked far away from the other wagons, so shouting for help would be useless.

But then, baby Isabella cried out loud. Her mother tried to quiet her, dropped the knife, and held her, but she kept crying louder and louder. One of the wolves crashed into the wagon's door. Isabella's mother, holding the infant tight, cried for help as the wolf continued its relentless onslaught until, finally, the door burst open. She stepped back, terrified, clutching her baby tighter. She dropped to the floor as the animal pounced, curling into a ball to protect the child. The wolf's fangs bit into her back, but all she cared about was protecting Isabella until help arrived, and finally, it did. They reached her wagon and killed one of the wolves with an axe. The second wolf bolted, and despite giving chase, they were unable to catch it. They could not save Isabella's mother. She had given her life to save her baby's.

Isabella was taken care of by her father's clan. They looked after her and ensured the baby girl didn't stroll too far from the camp – hiding her away whenever they heard a wolf howl. The curse, it appeared, was intense and persistent. They travelled from one place to another, crossing hills, valleys, and rivers, until one day, the howling stopped. They had reached the furthest land they could and camped there at World's Edge.

Early one morning, little Isabella wandered away from camp while the others slept. She was playful, curious, and stubborn, and, despite their warnings, she crossed the woods and reached the village. Isabella stopped near a cottage.

In the cottage lived a childless old farmer and his wife. Their hair had turned grey years ago, and they knew they would never be parents. They accepted it, but they never were truly happy. The old farmer felt sorry for his wife because he left her alone in the cottage every morning and went to farm the fields all day. One morning he found Isabella playing in front of the cottage. She wasn't from the village – he knew that much – from her clothes, he could tell she was a gypsy. However, she was a beautiful gypsy child. Her pretty face, dangling earrings, hair braids and ballerina shoes made her irresistibly adorable. She smiled at him, and his heart smiled back. He took Isabella's hand, carried her back to the woods, and found the camp. He asked for her mother and father, but they told him wolves killed them. He was deeply touched by this and kissed Isabella on her forehead before handing her to the gypsies. However, she did not want to let go of him and sobbed as he walked away. The farmer couldn't stand hearing her cry, and, seeing her arms outstretched for him, he stopped, turned back, and spoke with emotion.

'I could take her to my wife,' he said to one of her clan. 'She could look after her all day and keep her safe in our cottage. She spends the day with nothing to do, and she will be glad to look after her if you don't mind. We will be more than happy to help.'

He had no idea what he was doing or saying, but the words just came out. He felt foolish for asking such a thing. Maybe he had offended the gypsies, but it was too late to step back now, and he had to wait for their answer.

After a moment that felt like a decade to him, they agreed. He couldn't imagine why. He didn't know that they thought Isabella might be safer with him at the cottage. They hoped if she stayed there for a while, the curse might lose track of her, and the wolf would never find her again. They gave him Isabella and sent her clothes to the cottage. He was delighted, and so too was his wife. She loved Isabella as if she was her own. They cared for her, nurtured her, played with her, loved her, and she loved them back.

When it was time for the gypsies to travel and carry on their endless journey, the farmer and his wife were devastated, and Isabella didn't want to leave. She cried out and held on firmly to the farmer's wife, they even tried to pull her away gently, but she never let go. The farmer took a leap of faith and asked the gypsies if Isabella could stay and live with them. They would be her new family, and he promised to look after her as he would his own daughter.

Pressured by the plaintive cries of the child, the gypsies considered his request. Maybe it was safer for her, especially since the wolf didn't show up here at all, perhaps it was the right thing to be done, and she was meant to be here, in World's Edge. They saw the love Isabella held for the old farmer and his wife and believed maybe one of the travellers was meant to settle down. The gypsies agreed, allowing the old farmer and his wife to raise Isabella after telling him they would stop by to check on her yearly during the full moon festival. They also stressed that she remained free to leave the cottage and rejoin the tribe anytime.

Delighted, the farmer gave the gypsies his word, and they

shook hands. 'She is safe with us,' he assured them as he and his wife cried happy tears and held Isabella tightly.

And so, there she was, the village's gypsy girl. Year after year, the gypsies stopped by every full moon festival and opened their arms to Isabella, but she never chose to leave her new family. She settled down but remained a gypsy at heart. The way she dressed, her stone rings, earrings, and ballerina shoes screamed gypsy. She grew into a stunning young woman with a glowing smile, ebony hair and sparkling black eyes complimented by long eyelashes. Freckles dotted across her nose and dimpled cheeks – her attractiveness unparalleled within the village. Young men fell for her, enchanted by her beauty, but only one man captured her heart – the Merchant.

He ran to her. There were no receptions, protocols, or gifts for kings and queens. It was Isabella and only Isabella on his mind and in his heart.

He found her walking on the roads of the old village, carrying a basket full of red roses.

'Isabella,' the Merchant called to her as he approached. She turned and stunned him with a smile.

'I missed you,' the Merchant said and pulled her close as she wrapped her arms around him.

'I missed you, too,' she said as she sank into his chest. He tapped the basket hanging from her arm. 'Are you selling these?' She smiled. 'No.' Stepping away from him, she skipped off.

The Merchant caught up with her. 'Where are you going?'

'Come along,' Isabella said. 'You'll see.'

The Merchant frowned but followed her in silence as his thoughts grew loud. He felt like shouting his words, but he knew it was no use, for he already knew the answer to all his questions. They were in love, but she had never given in to him. Their relationship felt like a chase, committed but not submitted. Close, but not touching. She never pushed him away, yet never truly allowed him in. It was agonising, but he adored her. The more he knew her, the more he loved her. This daring gypsy flame never failed to spark his passion. A stubborn wild beauty of nature, he would never stop chasing and loving. He followed her, watched her, and everything he witnessed watered the deep roots of her love in his heart.

She ambled along the village roads, only stopping to hand the elderly and poor – who sat by the side – a single rose to each of them with a warm smile.

'What are you doing?' the Merchant asked as he walked next to her.

She paused. 'Well, I usually give them bread, but today I don't have any to give.'

He took hold of her hand. 'My fleet will dock soon, and they will have gold and silver coins. You don't have to—'

She pulled her hand free. 'Stop it! Not again.'

'I can take care of the poor, Isabella, and you know that.'

She placed a hand on his cheek. 'I know you can take care of their material needs, but look …' She pointed at an old blind woman touching the rose and smiling. 'I also take care of their hearts.'

'What about taking care of my heart, too?' he said as she gave out the last rose.

She turned to him. 'And how would that help?'

The poor – heading for the docks – ran past the pair.

He took hold of her. 'Come with me,' he shouted.

'No,' she said and wrestled herself free. 'Not before you tell me everything about yourself.'

'I have told you.'

'You haven't told me everything!' She turned and stormed off down the road.

The Merchant hurried after her and took hold of her arm again. 'You know I can't tell you everything. What I told you must be enough.'

She scoffed. 'Enough? Do you expect me to come with you, leave everything and everyone behind, hand you my life, and join your world without knowing everything about you? Without knowing where you are from? How did you get all that …' She pointed at the fleet. She stepped close and held his face in her hands. 'I don't even know your real name. I must know the man I am in love with. I need to fall in love with who you are, not who I think you might be. I need to know.'

The Merchant lowered his head and stepped back. 'You know I love you.'

'And I love you, but not … I want to love you fully, but I can't without knowing you completely.' She turned away from him. 'I can't … I just can't.' Isabella folded her arms together. 'If you want my unconditional love, then you must be real to me. I will not allow myself to fall deeper in love with some fleet, even if it is a thousand ships, even if it is the Merchant's.' She hurried inside and slammed the door.

Chapter 20

Clouds hung heavily over the sea. The sun was long gone, and the temperature had dropped, leaving a chill in the air. The old keeper stood, walked to a small closet, picked up some wool clothes, and turned to the sailor. "Put these on. You need warmer clothes."

"But I have some already." The sailor fished inside his bag.

The old keeper tossed the clothes into the sailor's lap. "You'll need more, trust me. It never hurts to have extra warm clothes."

"But what about you?"

"Don't worry, I have plenty," the old keeper said. He lit a small hand lamp and placed it on the wooden table in the middle of the room.

"Don't you get lonely here? How do you stand being here all alone?"

The old keeper chuckled. "The sea is open, and so is my door. Ships pass by, and I meet people. But believe it or not, I always have something to do. It keeps me busy and from getting lonely. I fix things, read, write, paint, and think. I have something to do every day." He wandered across to the window and stared outside. "But today …" He returned to his chair, sat, and wrapped a blanket around himself. "Today, I tell a story."

…

Chapter 21

After leaving Isabella, the Merchant made his way to see the old king. Of all the kings the Merchant visited, this king insisted on receiving the Merchant himself. He would stand at the castle gate when the Merchant visited, regardless of his ailing health. The king trudged to the gate and waited.

The guards announced the Merchant's arrival as he marched up to the old king and bowed. 'I am grateful for your generosity, your Grace. I would have gladly come to the throne room.'

'How could I not welcome you myself?' He opened his arms. 'You are like a son to me. My house is your house.'

He was a lone king, the last line of his house, with no sons nor kin. His castle was small and humble, just like his whole kingdom. A village, a small fleet of ships, and a modest army were all he possessed. What kept his kingdom safe – and the avaricious lands beyond – was its remote location and the formidable weapons his army had. The weapons were unbreakable yet light and fashioned from a unique metal found in his lands.

'Are they ready?' the Merchant asked.

The old king smiled. 'I knew you wouldn't wait for later. They are ready.' He motioned for his guest to follow him inside the castle towards the stables, where several rectangular wooden boxes lay one on top of the other.

The old king nodded, and the guards opened one of the boxes

before stepping back to allow the Merchant to view its contents. His eyes widened as he stared down at the swords inside. He lifted one up and gazed at it. The blade was light and long, made of a blueish metal that sparkled as a brief ray of sunlight coruscated from it. But once the sun had passed, and they now stood in the shade, it still glinted and gleamed.

The old king plucked one of the weapons from the box. 'You can split a rock into two with one of these,' he said, swinging the sword in a wide arc.

'What about the spears and arrows?'

'They are not ready yet, but soon will be,' the old king said. He smiled. 'The liquid you gave us was useful. It made our already incredibly strong weapons even stronger when we added it to the alloy. They are indestructible.' The king tapped his chin. 'Oh, that reminds me, how could I have forgotten? The swords must be treated before use, or they will rust and weaken like any other. They are fine here on land but can't be taken to sea for long periods unless treated first.'

'How?' the Merchant asked.

The old king took a small sack from the box, pulled a handful of green powder from it, and turned to the Merchant. 'Bury it in the sands ….' The king coughed and then continued. 'Bury the weapons with some of this powder but keep the hilt up and exposed to the salty air and sunlight for seven days.'

The Merchant widened his eyes. 'Sunlight? The sun rarely shows up from behind the clouds that shade World's Edge.'

'Find a place with people you can trust who live in a …' The old king coughed again. '… a sunny place, but keep the swords boxed until you arrive. Travel with them sealed.' The old king coughed once more, but this time more forcibly. He moved across to an unopened box and slumped onto it.

The Merchant took a small bottle out of his pocket and handed it to the king. 'Here, this will help you.'

'Thank you,' the old king said and took a small sip.

'The only kingdom with a sunny shore, who I trust, are the Silvers, but they are months away. If so, I must leave now to catch the sun.'

'Then do,' the old king said.

'But the arrows and the spears are not ready yet.'

'They will be when you return. Leave immediately, bury the blades, as I instructed, and come back for the arrows and spears.'

The Merchant pondered this. It wasn't the effort of the long journey back and forth that he was thinking about. It was her. He was thinking about Isabella, his beloved.

Chapter 22

That night, the whole village gathered in the square for the gypsies' full moon festival. A hush descended as everyone gathered around the large bonfire to see Isabella dance – something she had done for many years.

She made her way to the centre, through the crowd, and stood in front of the towering flames. She looked captivating, with two blue ribbons hanging loosely from her hair. Her full-length red and white chequered skirt and white cotton peasant blouse shimmered against the fire as it danced behind her, and a burgundy-coloured scarf billowed in the draft from the flames. She readjusted her high-waisted black belt, stretched a ballerina shoe-covered foot out and bent forward, leaning with one hand on her foot while the other held onto a moon-shaped tambourine. The crowd quieted further until only the crackling of the bonfire remained. She lifted her head a little – the black curls covering her face – and stood still.

The Merchant stood on the green hills watching Isabella with his eyes and heart. It was a fresh and beautiful night. The dew-covered grass glistened as the sea breeze blew gently under the full moon.

Isabella tapped on the tambourine, raising her head slowly with every tap. When upright, she raised her tambourine, rattled the jingles rapidly, and then stopped and looked down. The crowd cheered, and the music started playing. She danced around the fire with gypsy, blood-flamed moves. Her hair cascaded behind her as her steps and eyes captured the hearts and souls of the audience. She swirled and swirled while the Merchant stood uphill – deep in thought – watching her as his feelings grew stronger. She danced and smiled as he watched until he could bear it no longer. A strong urge coursed through him, and he strode downhill. Making his way through the throng, the Merchant burst into the circle of people and grabbed Isabella, pulling her away from the crowd. As the music played on, he led her up the green hills to the village. He stood before her beneath the glowing moon as she stared at him, panting.

He gazed into her eyes. 'If you want to know everything, I will tell you. I will let you know everything.'

The Merchant pulled Isabella close to his chest, rested his chin over her shoulder, and whispered his deepest secrets, his best and worst.

She listened intently as he spoke. She smiled, then frowned and widened her eyes as her mouth dropped open. She attempted to break free from him, but he held her firm, continuing to whisper. Telling her the deepest and darkest secrets he possessed. She ceased struggling as her body sagged, and with tear-filled eyes, she wrapped her arms around him and hugged him tightly.

'Hush,' she said softly as she ran her fingers through his hair, tears tumbling down her face. She gazed up at the sky.

He stopped whispering, stepped back, and looked her in the eyes. 'Now you know, Isabella. You know everything you wanted to know. I am far from perfect and could never be. Yet, I know you are not perfect and could never be. I adore you though I know that you are not all roses and cream, you are not as delicate as a butterfly or sweeter than honey, and I know you may not be the most beautiful woman in the world, but nothing is beautiful without you.'

He opened his arms wide, and she ran to him, rested her head over his shoulder and closed her eyes. 'I love you too,' she said.

He held her, then scooped her into his arms and carried her downhill to the shore and the sea.

Chapter 23

The Merchant took Isabella's hand and walked her around the main deck. She couldn't believe it. The ship's main deck was greater than anything she imagined it would be. He showed her his house, which was not a cabin as she expected, but a two-floor building. He showed her the baking area, the barns, the poultry, and the kettle ships.

It, indeed, was like a small village floating on water. They moved from one ship to another using planks and lines. She was excited. At some point, she slipped her hand out of his and skipped in front of him like a little girl, smiling back at him from time to time. He was stunned by her. Every minute, every day, every hour he spent in her company, he fell deeper in love. She owned his heart as no other could. For she was like no other. She was Isabella.

She grinned at him. 'I could have never imagined this.'

'Welcome to Venus,' the Merchant said as he took her hand to the main deck.

'So, the stories are true,' she said as she slowly pirouetted. 'It is a village on the waters. Is it also true that your fleet never breaks up, even in the worst storms? It holds formation no matter what?'

'Yes. My ships always hold formation.'

'How?'

He smiled at her. 'Skilled sailors and fine ships.'

She stepped closer to him. 'And is it true that you have never let any woman board the ship before?'

'It is. No woman has ever boarded Venus. Only you. I was waiting for you, and now you are finally here.' The Merchant grabbed her waist, pulled her close and spoke quietly in her ear. 'And some of the other stories are true.'

Isabella gazed up at him. 'What other stories?'

'Come. I will show you. You must see it for yourself.' The Merchant took her hand and led her down to the lower deck. Down and down they descended until they reached the lowest. He stopped, plucked a golden key from his belt, and opened the door.

Isabella strained to see in the darkness. 'Where are we?'

'Wait,' he said. He struck a match, lit a lamp, and then held it up for Isabella to view inside. She gasped. The room was full of gold. More gold than she could have ever imagined, even in her wildest dreams. The whole of the lower deck was full of gold. Chests overflowing with gold coins, gold bars and ingots.

'Welcome to Venus' belly,' the Merchant proudly said as he stood behind Isabella.

'You must be the richest man in the world,' she said.

'I am all yours forever, Isabella.' He walked to a nearby chest, took a tiara and placed it on her head.

'What is it?' she asked.

'It is your crown.'

'Crown?' She pulled it from her head. 'Crowns are for kings and queens, and I am not a queen.'

The Merchant smiled at her. 'You are a queen now. You are my queen.'

She gazed into his eyes. 'You don't have to give me gifts. It is not what you place on my head, around my neck or fingers that matters to me, but what you put in my heart.' She took hold of his hand and placed it on her chest. 'You have given me your love. That is all that matters.'

The Merchant took the tiara from her hand and placed it back on her head as he gazed into her eyes.

Isabella embraced him. 'Even if it was made of straws, I still would have worn it because it is a gift from my one and only love.' She closed her eyes and melted into him.

Chapter 24

The First Man watched as the boxes containing the swords were loaded onto the ships. The fleet was almost ready to leave World's Edge and return to the Red Marbled Kingdom. He was happy to set sail back to Prima but a moment later he remembered that he would be leaving her ashore again. His heart ached. The thought was torturous. He desperately wanted to be with her and marry like the Merchant was marrying Isabella. But he had his duties to perform and consoled himself with the fact that after delivering the swords, the fleet would return to World's Edge, and the Merchant would marry Isabella. She would wait for the Merchant's return, as Prima would wait for him, and prepare for the wedding, where the Merchant would announce her the queen of the fleet. No woman had ever sailed the fleet, but the Merchant had made an exception for Isabella, and she would be joining the fleet and sailing the world.

Wait, he thought, the Merchant made an exception for Isabella. Perhaps he could make another exception for Prima. Then he could marry Prima, against her stubborn father's will, and live onboard, just like Isabella. He smiled. I am the First Man, and I am entitled to an exception too. The Merchant would agree. He will make the exception, I am sure.

Hope made his assumption very convincing. The First Man smiled as he assured himself.

The Merchant will understand and make the exception.

He definitely will.

The First Man's thoughts were interrupted by the Merchant's voice.

'All set?' the Merchant said as he strode towards him.

The First Man pointed to the box being carried up the gangplank. 'That's the last one.'

'And the powder?' the Merchant said.

'On board, sir.'

'Good. We will set sail at the break of dawn.'

The First Man frowned. 'Won't we anchor for another day before we sail?'

'We don't have time,' the Merchant said. 'Sometimes, we have to make an exception.'

The First Man smiled. 'Yes, I believe so too,' he said under his breath and watched the Merchant descend the gangplank to the shore.

Chapter 25

During a standoff and a cold war between two kingdoms, spies became the most lethal weapon. Guards kept the borders and the gates tightly secured, especially the borderline that separated the two kingdoms. No one from either side was allowed to cross the line.

However, one Silver crossed the line freely. The guards helped him in and out but behind their commander's back. That person was a sixteen-year-old mute kid.

The guards never considered him a threat because he was mute. To them, letting him in and out was not even a breach of the rules. It was just an exception that took place behind their commander's back out of courtesy and nothing more. However, the main reason they did so was that he smuggled silver rings, bracelets and chains for the Silvers – something they were renowned for – and also other goods from the port. The Silvers' port was a commercial seaport, and none of the Red guards had access to it. The Mute smuggled goods and sold these to the Red guards, and he managed to set up his little black market that suited the Reds. They also liked him. He was funny, cheerful, and playful, and joked around and made them laugh. They never viewed him as a threat.

As usual, the Mute entered the Red guards' barracks, sat on the ground, and laid all the goods on a piece of cloth for display. The Red guards chose what they liked and offered him a price. If the Mute accepted the price, he nodded. If not, he shook his head and waved his hand. The guards were fair, though, and always gave him a good deal because they knew the Mute would leave and never return if they didn't. He was their window to the world behind the seas.

One day, after he made his sales, the Mute packed and made his way back to the Silver Kingdom. Just a few steps from the Red guards' barracks, the Commander and some royal guards showed up unexpectedly.

The Commander inspected the barracks, looked towards the gate and spotted the Mute walking out.

'Who is that?' the Commander asked. 'What is that kid doing here?'

The guard couldn't answer.

He glared at the guard. 'I said, who is that boy?'

'He is … he is … just a trader, Commander.'

'A trader? Traders trade in the market. What is he doing here?'

'We buy some stuff … and …' the guard said. 'He is a mute.'

The Commander growled. 'Mute or not, he still is a Silver, isn't he? Guards,' he shouted. And in a blink of an eye, the royal guards swarmed the place. 'Kill them all for treason.'

The Line guards drew their swords, and the fight began.

'Traitors!' The Commander shouted. Then, turning his attention back to the boy, who was now making his way uphill, he grabbed a bow and arrow and took aim at the Mute.

The Mute, who was walking and hopping across the rocks, happy with the day's earnings, didn't hear the arrow whistle through the air but stopped as it landed next to his foot. The Mute gazed at it, then spun around. His mouth fell open as he spotted the guards being cut down by the royal guards and the Commander taking aim at him. The Mute dropped his cloth sack and ran as fast as he could, zigzagging his way up the hill as one arrow after another narrowly missed him.

He stumbled and fell onto his knees as an arrow hit him between his shoulder blades. He groaned and fell forward onto the ground.

The Commander smiled. 'To hell with your spies.'

The Silver guards, who had witnessed what had happened, picked up their bows, ready to fire, but their officer shouted, 'Hold your arrows.' The guards lowered their bows.

'We don't want to start a war here,' the officer said. 'Go and get the child but lay down your weapons and go unarmed.'

Chapter 26

The Merchant's fleet sailed towards the Silver Kingdom as the First Man paced the main deck. It was sunset, and the breeze was light and fresh. He watched as the Merchant, leaning on a ledge, gazed at the horizon.

The First Man approached the Merchant and stood next to him. 'Homesick?' the First Man said.

The Merchant chuckled. 'Don't you know that the sea is my home?'

'Home is where the heart is, and your heart is with Isabella back on land.'

'She won't stay in World's Edge that long,' the Merchant said. 'Once we have dropped off the weapons, we'll sail back.'

'Won't we stop by the Red Kingdom as we always do?'

The Merchant turned to his junior. 'Not this time. We'll greet them when we return to pick up the weapons from the Silvers' shore.'

Another exception, the First Man thought and cleared his throat. 'I have been thinking, I mean, I wanted to ask you if … well …'

'What is it?' the Merchant said.

'I am in love.'

The Merchant patted his arm and smiled. 'Who is she?'

'Prima.'

'The Minister's daughter? That is why you are eager to get to the Red Kingdom. What did you want to ask me? Do you want to leave the fleet?'

The First Man lowered his head. 'I have been in the fleet my whole life, and leaving would be a tough step for me.'

'It will happen sooner or later. Will it not?'

'Well, someday, but I can't take this step now.' He coughed again. 'So, I was wondering if you'd make another exception for Prima and allow her onboard like—'

'As I did with Isabella?'

'Yes, sir.'

The Merchant gazed at the receding sun as it sunk below the horizon, then looked directly at the First Man. 'Isabella is an exception,' he said. 'If an exception is repeated, it becomes a rule, and soon every man aboard will ask the same. I do not intend to turn this fleet into a family-packed carrier.' He thrust his hands behind his back. 'I cannot help you with this. It is just out of the question. It could unbalance the fleet.'

The First Man frowned, and the Merchant narrowed his eyes. 'I don't understand,' the Merchant said. 'Why don't you settle with her on land. Back at the Red Kingdom?'

'Her father, the Minister, refuses to allow us to marry. I am not worthy enough.'

'Then, take her away, and marry in some other land.'

The First Man sighed. 'When it comes to his daughter, nowhere on land is out of his reach. He will seek us out, no matter how far we go. I will not be able to stop him from taking her back. After all, he is the Red Kingdom's Minister. But he would not dare to touch your fleet.'

'I am sorry to hear that, but as I explained …' The Merchant nodded at his junior officer and marched off.

The First Man followed him. 'There is another solution.'

The Merchant stopped. 'And what would that be?'

'If I am rich enough, her father will accept and bless our marriage. If I leave the fleet and settle down with Prima on land …' He looked away. 'Would I get my share of gold?'

'Of course,' the Merchant said, 'like any of my men. You would get a share of gold.'

'No, that is not what I meant. My rightful share of gold,

not a share of the gold. As the First Man, surely I am entitled to an equal share of all the gold in Venus' belly.'

The Merchant scoffed. 'What? An equal share? You know the rules. An equal is only given to the first man at the fleet's dismantlement. You know that. You have been a loyal First Man. I can give you a hefty share of gold now, and if the fleet ever dismantles, I will bring you the rest of your share myself, wherever you are. I have never broken a promise. You agreed to this when you joined my fleet. Need I remind you?'

'No, sir, but matters are different now. Prima's father will only give me her hand in marriage if I am rich. I implore you.'

'You will be well-off with the share of gold I will give you,' the Merchant said.

'Yes, it will make me comfortable, but not wealthy enough to win her father's approval. However, if I get an equal share of gold, I'll be as rich as any nobleman. Only then can I buy a castle with sufficient land to impress her father. Only then would he be happy to give me her hand in marriage.'

The Merchant glared at him. 'A share of gold is all I can offer. If it is insufficient, you will have to find another solution.' The Merchant turned and strode off.

The First Man scowled at the Merchant as he watched him disappear. He was angry. It was bad enough to be parted from his beloved while at sea, but the thought of losing her for good was too much to bear. He groaned and brought his fist down hard on the handrail.

Chapter 27

Back in the narrow streets of the Silvers' village, in a run-down cottage, the mute boy's mother dried the beads of sweat from her son's forehead. He had been feverish and unconscious since the arrow that had wounded him was removed. She watched him start to shiver again and gently touched his neck with her hand. The fever was getting higher, and he began to mumble in his sleep.

She rushed to the table next to the bedroom window, picked up and opened a small crystal bottle containing an orange liquid, and dripped a few drops on his lips. He was breathing heavily and shivering more as she returned. She didn't know what else to do and felt helpless. That liquid was the only thing keeping her son alive – a medicine that the Merchant had given her long ago and instructed her to give any of her children should they fall ill. She had kept the bottle safe. Now its usefulness was apparent. The local physician had shaken his head and given her no hope, informing the crying woman that it was unlikely the boy would last more than an hour. But here he was, still alive, and with the long, wearisome night behind her, her optimism had risen. She prayed with all her heart for the Merchant to return soon as her medicine wouldn't last much longer, and perhaps he would provide more help to the stricken boy. She was confident he was the only one who could heal him. She clasped his hand and kissed it, uttered a prayer and waited.

Chapter 28

The sea was calm at the edge of dawn, and the Merchant's fleet was quiet. Most of the crew were still in their cabins, including the Merchant. The main mast's man climbed up the pole adroitly, grabbed one of the hanging horns and, standing high overlooking the whole fleet, took a deep breath and blew the horn. The crew roused themselves as they recognised the sound well. A crew member was dead.

The Merchant hurried from his house and stood in front of it. Some of the gunner crew climbed the stairs behind the house and strode towards him. The men stopped and bowed their heads.

'Who is it?' the Merchant asked a man standing before him.

'It is the head gunner, sir.'

The gravity of the loss showed on the Merchant's face. The head gunner was one of the oldest members of the fleet, and for many years he had served the Merchant well with his top-notch fire skills. No one ran a fire floor as he did. He was old yet in good health, and nobody expected a sudden death. The Merchant sat and pondered. Venus couldn't sail without a skilled head gunner, and he knew that none of the current crew could handle ninety guns on Venus alone as well as the head gunner had. He exhaled a deep breath and stood. 'Anchor the ships and get ready for the funeral. Get Ji Kai.'

Chapter 29

The sailor shifted in his chair. "Ji Kai?" he said to the old keeper.

"Yes. A venerable Chinese man. Traditional in every way. Wise, calm and self-assured. Dressed in his full traditional Chinese costume, he was a sight to behold. None of the Merchant's crew had been on board before him. Some say he was the first one the Merchant recruited into his fleet. Some say he was more than a hundred years old but had the strength of a twenty-year-old. He had long hair, completely white. It dangled from the top of his head to the back of his knees." The old keeper smiled. "He was quiet and rarely talked. He never shared a square or a bed with any of the sailors and lived on a separate ship all alone. His mystical presence and old age made the sailors curious and cautious around him. They would even avoid eye contact, but they often stared at him from a distance as he meditated every morning at sunrise. Ji Kai was also the Merchant's head healer, and because he was the oldest crew member, he was the one to carry out funeral ceremonies."

"I bet their funeral ceremonies differed from all others," the sailor said.

"Yes. Very different. Very quiet."

"Do you know the details?" the sailor said, his eyes widening. "Could you tell me about it?"

The old keeper smiled and nodded.

Chapter 30

The Merchant's fleet anchored in the middle of the sea as all the high-ranking officers and men lined up aboard Venus. The gunners stood in a circle around the head gunner's body, which lay on a wooden table. His body had been carefully prepared. After washing him, rare aromatic oils had been rubbed into his skin. The Merchant stood alone on the plank, and the sailors watched from their ships as they all silently waited for Ji Kai.

Ji Kai climbed the stairs behind the Merchant's house that led to Venus' main deck in slow, steady steps. As soon as he walked aboard, everyone standing in place stepped backwards as a sign of respect. Ji Kai strode slowly forward and stood next to the head gunner's body, then took a small bottle out of his pocket, opened it, and handed it to one of the youngest gunners standing in the circle. He took the bottle from Ji Kai and whispered one word to the liquid inside it, then handed it to the one next to him. In turn, they all whispered a word to the bottle and passed it along until it was returned to Ji Kai. He closed the bottle and placed it in his pocket. Then, lifting the head gunner's body into his arms, he made his way to the plank. At that point, everyone bent a knee and lowered their eyes, except the Merchant, who waited for Ji Kai to approach. The Merchant looked down at the head gunner's body, wrapped in the finest linen, and unwrapped the head, exposing his face, before whispering a word into his ear. Ji Kai then walked the length of the plank, carrying the head gunner's body, paused briefly at the end, and allowed it to roll free from his arms and into the waters. The body hit the water with a splash and headed downwards towards the seabed, as Ji Kai took out the bottle from his pocket, opened it and poured the remaining contents into the same spot as the body. Then, picking up a long rope tied to a plank, he threw the loose end into the waters. Ji Kai uttered words no one understood as he tossed the empty bottle into the sea. Everyone stared at the rope dangling from the plank into the water …

… "What was the rope for?" the sailor said.

"Dropping the rope was essential to their rituals," the old keeper said. "The Merchant and crew believed the souls of the dead would climb up the line back to the ship. The line, as they called the rope, was the soul's way back to where it belonged – the fleet." …

… Ji Kai slowly made his way back to his ship, and the Merchant returned to his house. The gunners carried the wooden table and returned to their floors as, one by one, everyone left Venus' main deck until only the First Man was left and was the last to leave.

Chapter 31

The old keeper picked up his pipe and tapped the contents from it. "Let me tell you about the twins," he said, pushing fresh tobacco into the bowl.

"The twins?" the sailor said.

The old keeper nodded as he lit the pipe …

… The Mute's mother sat on the edge of his bed, feeling helpless. The life was being drained slowly from her son, and only the Merchant's medicine had kept him alive this long. But now she had dripped the last of the liquid onto the boy's lips. Her long-held dam of tears finally broke, and she wept, unable to stop herself as they cascaded relentlessly down her face. 'I am going to lose him,' she thought, 'Is it my fault? Have I been a horrible mother to him? Should I have never let my twins spy? Even if it was for the benefit of the kingdom?'

Yes, the Mute had a twin, and they were identical in looks and behaviour. However, the second twin wasn't mute. They were both born with full hearing, but one caught a fever that almost cost him his life. Nonetheless, the fever didn't spare his hearing, and he became deaf and mute as he grew older. The Silvers thought it would be a great trick to play on the Reds. Send them the Mute first, as a trader, a smuggler, and when they were assured that the boy couldn't hear anything around him and couldn't talk about anything he saw in the barracks of the Red Castle, his twin would replace him, every once in a while, they traded places. The trick worked well for a long time. They were out of the Red King's spies' sight, who had their eyes fixed on the Silver Castle and its soldiers. None of them paid attention to the poor peasants. 'Now my boy is dying, and I can't save him,' the mother muttered to herself, her grief limitless. 'Mother,' said her other son, standing at the door. She looked at him, worry etched deeply on her features. 'I have wonderful news,' he said. 'He is here. The Merchant has arrived.' She let out a cry and grasped her stricken son's hand as tears, this time joyful ones, ran down her face.

Chapter 32

She remembered people shouting, 'The widow gave birth! The widow gave birth!' How could she forget such a day? Such a moment when she gave birth to her twin boys. They handed her the newborns as tears of sadness and happiness poured out. Now a mother of two wonderful but fatherless children, for their father had died in a battle, defending the kingdom and protecting them. She never wished to have him next to her as much as she did that day. That moment when she heard people shouting, 'The widow gave birth!'

She felt helpless, fragile, insecure, and anxious, but she had toughened enough to raise them independently. But now and then, she broke down, and only one man lifted her back to her feet at such moments. The Merchant was her backbone, caretaker, and saviour. At the darkest times, he was her only light. The Merchant even taught the Mute a language, a sign language through which he could communicate and express himself. The Mute waved the words, and his brother spoke these words out. She still remembered the happy tears she cried when he waved his first sentence and his brother translated it for her. The sentence was, 'Mother, I love you.'

The Mute's mother and brother ran to the docks and were allowed onboard Venus. It was an impressive experience for anyone who dreamt of stepping aboard the legendary ship. Still, they were focused on the Merchant, awaiting his reply after the twin's mother heartily asked for his kind help.

The Merchant motioned to one of his men, and the man brought him a small wooden box. The Merchant opened it and inside sat six small glass bottles just like the one she possessed. But each of these had a liquid of a different colour – red, yellow, green, purple, black, and white.

'Healing will take time,' the Merchant said. 'He has been ill for quite a while, and you won't be able to treat him yourself. It will be too confusing for you and too risky for the child.' He turned to the First Man who stood next to him. 'The First Man will stay with you,' the Merchant said. 'He knows how to treat your son using the medicine correctly.' He looked the First Man in the eye. 'Stay with her and heal the Mute till we get back.'

The First Man nodded. 'At your command.' He felt happy to have the chance to see Prima, yet wasn't entirely comfortable with the Merchant's decision. He could have left a healer to treat the Mute. The First Man was skilled, yes, but why him and not a healer? Maybe it was a subtle penalty for crossing the line that day, or perhaps the Merchant was giving him time to rethink it all with Prima.

'Thank you, Merchant, thank you so much,' the Mute's mother said. The First Man accompanied her off Venus' main deck. She walked ahead in front of the First Man, who stood still for a moment and looked back at the Merchant.

The Merchant was leaning on the ledge, the sun was about to set, and the horizon was painted red. The Merchant watched the Silvers digging holes on the beach, emptying a handful of the green powder, sticking in the swords then filling the hole with sand. Hundreds of blades were buried up to the handle all along the shore. It looked somewhat beautiful yet intimidating – planted swords that only the reaper had to worry about. The First Man gazed at it all momentarily, then walked away. A sailor's heart could always sense when the winds were about to change. He walked along the shore, hearing the men shouting,

'Set sail … set sail!'

Chapter 33

Prima turned to her father as they were having dinner in their humble house. 'The First Man wants to meet you,' she said.

'Not again!' the Minister said, throwing his spoon onto the plate.

'Father, please. He is the one for me.'

The Minister scoffed. 'You say he is the one … but from where I sit, he isn't. I see it.' Prima stood, about to leave the table, but he grabbed her arm. 'So, what do you want me to do?' he continued. 'Stand here with a smile as I watch my only daughter ruin her life for someone not worthy of her. Is that what you want me to do? You are asking my permission to harm yourself, my only child.'

'I am not harming myself … you are the one who is harming me.' She pulled her arm away.

'Me?' the Minister stared open-mouthed. 'Listen, my darling—'

'No, Father, you listen. Do you believe every woman who marries a wealthy man is happy? When my mother married you, weren't you poor? Yet, she loved you. Was she miserable? No, she was happy, wasn't she?'

'But she ended up in misery,' the Minister shouted. 'No matter how much we loved each other, my love for her couldn't save her. She died because I couldn't afford to treat her. Love brought her to me … poverty took her away. I will never let that happen to you.'

'But we are rich. I don't need a wealthy man.'

'We are not rich nor powerful enough. We can't afford a castle.'

'I don't want a castle, Father.' She scowled at him. 'Who said I want to live in a castle? I hate them. Most of my life is spent inside one.'

Her father banged his fists on the table. 'Prima, once and for all. You are not marrying that sailor, no matter how much you think you love him or how much you think you hate castles. Understood?'

'All this because of what you think is right. Because you think you know what is best for me. You have no idea.' She stepped away and turned her head. 'If you have seen what I have seen in the hallows of that castle, you would never say that. I have seen the woman everyone thinks has it all. I have seen her cry in her sleep, the misery of loving one and living with another, and I will not let myself end up like that in some castle. I will not, and no one will force me to, not even you.'

His eyes narrowed. 'What do you mean?'

'Nothing,' Prima said, turning back to face him. 'I meant nothing.'

He stood and grabbed hold of her again, gripping her arm tightly. 'What did you say? Who are you talking about?'

'Nothing.' She squealed as he tightened his grip.

He shook her. 'Answer me!'

'Father, you are hurting me.'

'Answer me. Who is the woman you are talking about?'

'Please let go.'

He pulled her closer and pushed his face nearer. 'Answer me, damn you.'

'The Queen! It is The Queen!' she said. 'She doesn't love the Red King. She is in love with another man. She is heartbroken, and I will not live like that. I will marry the one I love.'

He shook her again. 'Who? Who does she love?'

'Father, let me go,' she pleaded as teardrops tumbled down

her cheeks.

'Who is he?' he bellowed.

'The Merchant! She loves the Merchant!'

The Minister released her arm, and Prima ran to her room.

He dropped back into his chair and pondered his daughter's words. Could what she had told him be true? He lifted his drink to his lips and took a sip of wine. This was the moment he had been waiting for. The Minister refilled his glass as a large grin spread across his face.

Chapter 34

The Red King lay on his back, staring at the ceiling, waiting for the Queen to come to bed as she finished brushing her hair. Taking good care of her long hair was a routine she never skipped, not on any night.

'Can you imagine that the Merchant has docked at the Silvers' and left on the same day without stopping by the castle to greet us?' the Red King said.

'That's a first,' the Queen said. 'But why is that? Do any of your spies know the reason?'

The Red King turned onto his right side to face her. 'Well, the word is he is getting married.'

The Queen stopped brushing her hair and spun around to face her husband. 'What?' she exclaimed.

'Can you imagine?' the Red King said. 'He turned back on the same day just to be with her ... to marry her. He is rushing back for his wedding. They say he is deeply in love, but of course, no one can love anyone as much as I love you,' he said and smiled at the Queen.

The Queen started to breathe heavily. 'And ... who is the lucky one?'

'A gypsy girl from World's Edge Kingdom. She will join the vessel. He put a tiara on her head and crowned her queen of his fleet.' The Red King laughed. 'A woman on board the fleet. He is breaking the rules for her.' The Queen scowled. The Red King narrowed his eyes. 'What's the matter? Are you all right, my love?'

'No. I am not.' She sprung to her feet. 'I will retire to my chamber,' she said and exited the royal suite, slamming the door behind her. The Red King frowned and stared at the door she had left by.

Chapter 35

The First Man sat opposite the Minister at the end of a table. Prima sat midway between the pair.

'Thank you for finally allowing me to meet you, Minister,' the First Man said. The Minister glared at him but remained silent.

Prima leant forward. 'He … … is staying with us … on land … for some months … until—'

The Minister held up his hand. 'So, you are the one who has my daughter's heart?'

'She has my heart, too. We are in love and want to spend the rest of our lives together.'

'Love isn't enough,' the Minister said and took a sip of his wine. 'Marriage is like building a house. If it is built on soft land, it will crumble. The hard surface of the reality you are escaping is what holds mountains up. Fall in love, both of you, as much as you want, but if you want to sustain that love, to protect it, it must be sheltered by thick hard walls and trust me, those thick hard walls are costly.'

The First Man leaned forward. 'I understand that you want the best for Prima, and that's what I want for her too. I will do everything I can to be the best for her.''

'And how do you intend to do that?' the Minister asked.

'Well, to begin with, I will leave the fleet and get a hefty share of gold then—'

'What? What share? What gold?' the Minister said.

Prima frowned. 'Yes, what gold?'

The First Man eased himself back in his chair. 'Every trade the Merchant profits from is shared with all his crew members in gold. Since I have been the fleet's first man for a long time, my share is enough to make me a wealthy man.' The Minister lowered his brow and studied the sailor.

Prima smiled. 'How come you never told me about this before?'

'I didn't want to jump ahead before clearing it with the Merchant himself. Just to be sure.'

'Well, that is good to hear, but how rich are we talking about here?' the Minister asked.

The First Man shuffled in his seat. 'Well, rich enough to start our married life.' The Minister leaned back in his chair and continued to study the First Man.

'But just for now,' the First Man spluttered. 'It is just a share. I'll be richer when I get my full share.'

'What do you mean?' Prima asked while the Minister stared and listened.

'If the fleet is dismantled, I will get my full equal share. An equal share of Venus' gold would make me as rich as the richest prince. There is enough gold in her belly to build a kingdom.'

The Minister smiled and leaned forward on the table. 'So, the stories are true. Venus' fat belly is loaded with gold?'

'More than you can imagine, sir,' the First Man said as Prima reached out and took hold of her beloved's hand. She turned and smiled at her father.

The Minister stood, turned his back to them, and pondered the First Man's words. He turned to face them again. 'Walk with me,' he said to the First Man. 'Prima, wait for us here. We are going outside.'

The Minister and the First Man strolled around the cottage. After taking a few steps, the Minister stopped. 'What did you mean by saying "if the fleet is dismantled?"'

'The Merchant has put in some rules,' the First Man said. 'There are certain conditions that, in some cases, dismantle the fleet. He doesn't intend to roam the seas forever after all.'

'And what are those conditions?'

'It is simple, either the Merchant orders the dismantlement himself or if … well … I'd rather not speak about the other condition.'

'I bet the second condition has to do with the Merchant's death, doesn't it?' the Minister said.

The First Man nodded. 'Yes, Minister, it does. That's why I'd rather not talk about it.'

'As you like.' The Minister smirked. 'If the fleet is ever dismantled …'

'When it is dismantled,' the First Man said.

'When would the Merchant ever order that?' the Minister asked.

'I'm not sure, but the Merchant has never broken a promise.'

'A promise with an open condition. It sounds like a fake promise to me,' the Minister said. 'Let me ask you this, have you ever seen the Merchant give out an equal share to anyone who has devotedly worked for him?'

'Not that I know of, but I am sure that—'

'And tell me, does that equal share exclude or include Isabella's share now? I heard he's given her a tiara.' The First Man said nothing as the Minister continued. 'Exactly.' The Minister stopped and looked the First Man in the eye. 'You are just finding comfort in the illusion of trusting the Merchant. A promise that has never been fulfilled and is left to sheer uncertainty is nothing but an illusion, and you are convincing yourself that such an illusion is real. Do you want me to leave my only daughter on the threshold of an uncertain future that will never be realised? If you want to marry Prima … get your equal share or get out of her life.' The Minister turned and strode back towards the cottage.

'But the fleet has to be dismantled first!' the First Man shouted after him.

The Minister stopped at the threshold, then marched back to the First Man. He placed a hand on his shoulder and grinned. 'I am a resourceful man, and I can help you get your equal share.'

The Minister laughed. 'Or even bigger than your so-called equal share.'

'What do you mean? How?' the First Man said.

'That is not the question you should be asking now. What you should be asking is how deeply you love Prima. And how far do you trust the Merchant?' the Minister walked a few steps away from the First Man, then turned back again. 'I think you know what I mean.'

Chapter 36

The Minister's words resounded in the First Man's head. How deeply did he love Prima, and how far did he trust the Merchant? How deeply do I love Prima? he thought. Then another thought entered his head. What made me fall in love with Prima in the first place? She was pretty. No, he corrected himself. She was beautiful. But it wasn't only her beauty that had attracted him. A woman's beauty is enough to grab a man's attention but not enough to make him fall in love with her. It was not only how she looked but what she promised. Her face promised beauty in every aspect, and she had fulfilled that promise. Her warmth, passion, tenderness, and subtle allure were beauty in manifestation. She was his mind's definition of beauty. So, how could he ever give her up? How could anyone give up such a beauty and drive her out of his life?

Beauty is the only thing we love, and wherever we see it, we hold on to it, whether it is a place, a thing, a state or, atop of all, a person. It is our only goal, all of us, but we see it differently. How much do I love Prima? He recalled the Minister's question. Love. What is love? It is a feeling. No, it is the only feeling. We feel nothing but love. Hate is the opposite of love … pain is losing what you love, jealousy is not having what you love, and loyalty is committing to what you love. The Merchant once told me that all colours come from one single ray of white light. Love is that white light for all our feelings. All our feelings are just a variation of love. Yes, we only feel love, and Prima is the only one I feel. That is how deeply I love Prima. That answers your question, Minister, the First Man concluded. But how far do I trust the Merchant? He had never broken a promise but had only fulfilled promises made through his perspective and judgment. And according to the Merchant's judgment, he couldn't have his equal share, even though it would mean losing Prima, the love of his life. According to his judgment, he could make an exception for Isabella and crown her queen of the fleet but wouldn't give him an equal share even if his life depended on it. Selfishness, he thought, was when one judges from their own perspective only. Which is what the Merchant always did. He trusted that he would keep his promises but didn't know how the Merchant judged things. Maybe it is time for me to judge, the First Man thought.

Chapter 37

Late at night, Prima couldn't sleep, and her father couldn't either. She stepped downstairs and found him sitting in front of the fireplace staring at his late wife's portrait. She looked beautiful in that painting.

'Sleepless?' he asked Prima, then sipped his drink.

She smiled. 'Yes.'

'You are sleepless here and in the Red Castle, too?' he said.

'I will sleep in the arms of the one I love,' she said.

The Minister smiled, then turned back to the painting with tear-filled eyes.

'Do you still love her?' Prima asked softly.

The Minister sighed. 'Every single moment I spend without her, I spend in agony. If it weren't for you, I wouldn't have been able to carry on.'

She placed her hand on his arm. 'I love you, Father.'

'And I love you too, darling. And I want you to be happy and live in love, like your mother and I.'

'Do you?' she said.

'I do. I do,' he said and turned to her. 'And I will help you.'

'Help me? How?'

'I can help you be with the First Man by assisting him in getting his gold.'

'Really?' She smiled, took hold of his hand, and sat beside him.

'Yes,' he said, 'but first, I need you to get me something

from the Red Castle.'

'What?'

'You said that the Queen writes love letters to the Merchant, right?'

'Yes, she does.'

'And the Merchant returns those letters to her?'

'He does,' she said.

He looked into her eyes. 'Does she keep those letters somewhere or burn them?' he said.

Prima frowned. 'She keeps them hidden in her chamber.'

'I knew she'd keep them!' His eyes widened. 'Do you know where she hides them? Can you get me one of those letters?'

Prima lowered her head. 'I'm not sure I …'

'All I need is one letter, and I will help you be with the First Man. He will be rich and wealthy then, and you both will have my endless blessing in your marriage.'

Someone knocked on the cottage's door.

'Who is that at such a late time?' Prima said.

The Minister smiled and stood. 'I bet I know who that is, and it is not too late. He is just in time.' The Minister put down his drink and opened the door. 'Welcome … son,' the Minister said to the First Man standing outside.

Chapter 38

The Black Collar entered the bar, nodded at the bartender, and walked directly behind the counter, through the door and down to the room below. The Minister was already there, waiting at a wooden table. As soon as he heard the Black Collar enter, he smirked. 'You are here.'

'You wanted to see me urgently. I believe you stressed the importance,' the Black Collar said as he took off his coat and hung it up.

'Yes,' the Minister said, then added, 'have a seat.'

The Black Collar sat and stared at the Minister, waiting for him to speak. When he didn't, he said, 'What did you want to see me for? Do you have a plan?'

The Minister smiled and leaned back in his chair. 'I want to see the Dean.'

'What, now?'

'You heard me.'

The Black Collar drummed his fingers on the arm of his chair. 'And why do you want to meet the Dean? If you don't mind me asking, Minister.'

'He will know himself when he gets here.'

'What? Are you out of your mind?' The Black Collar scoffed. 'Not only do you want to see the Dean in person, but to top it off, you want the Dean himself to come to you?'

The Minister folded his arms. 'Yes.'

The Black Collar narrowed his eyes at the Minister,

whose lips curled into a sneer. 'Even if I asked him to,' he stuttered, 'how would I convince the Dean to come to you here?'

The Minister stood and put his arms behind his back. 'Tell him that this is it.' The Minister walked over to the fireplace and stared into the flames. 'This is when and where we bring the Merchant down, once and for all.' He turned around and looked at The Black Collar.

The Black Collar stood and closed the gap between himself and the Minister. 'Do you have a plan?'

The Minister smiled. 'I have what's better than a plan. I have an ally from the inside. Tell the Dean that the Merchant is stronger than each of us, but he is not stronger than all of us.' He turned away from The Black Collar again. 'For it to happen, he has to be here, and it has to be now.'

Chapter 39

Two veiled men lay atop the highest hill and looked through telescopes at the swords spiked along the Silvers' shore. After studying them for some time, one of the veiled men put down the telescope, looked to the other and left. The other man followed.

The Red King and the Minister removed their veils as they entered the royal hall.

The Red King sat on his throne. 'Why didn't you tell me earlier?' he said, signalling for a drink.

'I wanted you to see for yourself, Sire,' the Minister replied.

The Red King sipped his drink. 'And now I have.'

'He is arming them, Sire … the Merchant is arming the Silvers.'

'You said the weapons are the Merchant's, not theirs. He didn't sell them to the Silvers, and even if he is arming them, no matter how strong those swords are, we will still crash them to the ground if they dare to venture downhill.'

The Minister furrowed his brow, and he stepped a little closer. 'Why are you doing this, Sire?'

'Doing what, Minister?' the Red King said, glaring at him.

'This.' The Minister threw his head back and growled. 'You do it every time. You find him a way out, an excuse … as if you dare not confront him.'

The Red King stood and tossed his drink aside. The vessel clattered across the stone floor before resting against the far wall. 'Have you lost your mind?' he screamed.

'May I speak to you in private?' the Minister asked.

'Speak to me in private?' The Red King took hold of the Minister and pushed him backwards. 'At this point, I wonder if I should allow you to address me at all.'

'Your Highness, I beg you. I meant no disrespect.'

The Red King signalled for his guards and servants to leave the royal hall. When the last one left and shut the door, the Red King stepped over to the Minister and pushed his face closer. 'Are you deliberately testing my patience? Because if you are, I must warn you, I have none.'

The Minister edged back and lowered his head. 'So why are you so patient with the Merchant?'

The Red King rolled his eyes. 'Again? Why does this matter to you that much? What difference does it make anyway?'

'You know the difference between him and us?' the Minister said.

The Red King sat and waved a dismissive hand at his Minister. 'What?'

'Them!' The Minister walked across to the window and pointed outside. 'Our people, the guards, the Silvers, the children, all of them! They love him more than any of us … more than you, your Highness, more than the Queen herself … they talk about him, praise him … wait for him by the shore … he owns them. They are his.' The Minister stepped back across to the King. 'He sails the sea with an army bigger than any on land. He has weapons that no one can beat … weapons made of metal no one has seen before. He has enough cannons to light up the night sky. I ask you this, Sire. Would he keep roaming the seas, curing people, and helping everyone without asking for anything in return? No, my king, of course not. He is just waiting for the right moment. He has already won … strategically. He has already defeated our soldiers with his own. He has beaten our cannons with his. When the time is right, he will take over the kingdom with a snap of his fingers, and you know what? They …' He pointed a finger towards the window. '… they won't mind. Because they love him. Throughout my serving years, I have learnt that one shouldn't fear the strongest in arms but rather the most loved in hearts. The hearts of your enemy, the hearts of your people and above all, the heart of all hearts … the heart … of your Queen.'

The Red King's eyes widened, and his mouth dropped open. The Minister laid one of the Queen's love letters before the Red King. 'Read this, Sire, and you will understand.'

The Red King picked up the letter and read it. He slowly shook his head as his face reddened. He looked across at the Minister, his hands shaking as he gripped the letter.

The Minister made a fist with his right hand. 'Let's take him down, Sire. Let us break him once and for all and end all this.'

The Red King looked at him through tear-laden eyes as the Minister edged closer. 'I have a plan. No matter how powerful he is, no matter how many men he has or how strong his weapons are, I have the plan to bring him down. I've always planned to protect your throne. I have always looked after your crown and your father's. The Red Kingdom shall prevail by the loyalty of its followers. Always.'

The Red King stared at the letter in his hand as the Minister continued, 'There is a force, a blind spot, one the Merchant does not account for. I had to find a new, unexpected way to carry out the plan. After all, the enemy of our enemy is a friend. Hundreds of pirate ships are on the seas. One thinks they are astray, but they are all governed by one family, and I have established contact with them. They are the only ones who can bring the Merchant down in return for a mutual benefit. They are named The Blacks, Sire.' Still, there was no reaction from the Red King – his head now bowed. 'I know it is overwhelming, Sire. You must take your time, but let's not lose this opportunity. The Merchant's first man is on our side … he wants to bring the Merchant down. See? Even the closest to the Merchant knows the threat he poses.' The Minister paused, then added, 'I will be at my house, Sire. Make your decision, and I will be at your service. But for now, I suggest that no one knows anything about this, not even the Queen. Especially the Queen.'

The Minister walked out, leaving The Red King alone in the

royal hall, and as he headed away from the palace, a broad smile spread across his face.

Chapter 40

The Red King remained in the royal hall until the next day. He didn't sleep, didn't eat, didn't drink, and didn't allow anyone in.

At dawn, he called for his guards and asked them to summon the Minister, who rushed to the Red Castle and stood before the Red King.

'Sire …' he said. The Red King stood by a narrow window, still holding the letter and didn't answer.

'Shall I call the Blacks?' the Minister asked, but still, the Red King didn't answer. He silently, gazed outside into his kingdom. His knuckles whitened as he balled his hands into fists.

The Minister hesitated as he appraised the Red King, but summoning his courage, he stepped closer. 'My King,' he said louder. 'Shall I call for the Blacks?' The Minister waited, and the Red King finally nodded.

The Minister smiled and raised his chin as a huge grin spread across his face. He bowed and left. The Red King turned and watched the Minister leave the throne hall.

A carriage pulled by four jet-black horses made its way through the mists of the woods. As black as the horses, the carriage, topped with a crest of a black feathered crow, beak down, wings spread – the unmistakable crest of a family that has long worked in the shadows. The Red King sat on his throne, unaware the Blacks were already on their way.

Chapter 41

The black carriage stopped and hid in the woods while the Minister sneaked out of the Red Castle and ushered the unannounced guest into the royal court.

The Red King's unannounced guest was the Black family's Dean himself.

The Dean was an arrogant, egoistic, powerful, middle-aged man. Though it should have been the eldest to be Dean of the family, he became Dean because he was the most cunning, ruthless, manipulative man in the Black family. His looks also gave him the aura he needed to rule the family – an Albino with white skin, white hair and piercing blue eyes that one would not dare to look into. He dressed in black and wore the Black family's crest ring on his right index finger – made of black metal shaped in the image of a crow.

The Red King received the Dean in a secret meeting room in the Red Castle. They sat face to face and waited for the Minister to usher in the one person left who needed to attend and start laying out the plan. The Minister smiled as he opened the doors and presented their most vital ally. 'This is the Merchant's first man,' the Minister said.

The First Man glanced at the other people around the table and eased himself onto a chair. 'I …' He took a deep breath. '… I want half.'

'Half?' the Minister exclaimed.

'Half of the gold,' the First Man said.

The Dean stared at him. 'And why do you think you are entitled to half of the earnings?' he asked.

'Because it is not half of the earnings. When the Merchant is brought down, the seas will be open for your pirate ships, and you will make much more than you are making now.' He looked at the Red King. 'When the Merchant is out of the way, you will be able to rebuild the ships and take the furthest corner of the world under your sovereignty. The Red Kingdom will be the largest in the world, and you …' He turned to the Minister. '… You will be the minister of such a kingdom.' Then he turned to the three of them. 'You will all have that, plus your share of gold. But, I will only get the gold, so I am entitled to half of it because half of the gold is not half of the earnings.'

'You are correct,' the Dean said, 'if you are the only one who can bring down the Merchant, but I hear there could be other ways, too. Cheaper ways.'

The First Man scoffed. 'What other ways? Attack the fleet, shoot your cannons? See where that gets you.'

The Dean turned to the Red King. 'Yes. If placed on the Teardrop Isles, all our pirate ships, all the Red Kingdoms' cannons, would form a colossal fire force that could obliterate the Merchant's fleet.' The Dean sat back in his chair and sneered. 'We don't need you.'

The First Man smiled. 'But by then, you will not get the gold to cover the expenses. Making such an attack is too expensive for you without my help. It would only be a hollow victory.'

'What do you mean?' the Minister asked.

The First Man turned to the Minister. 'If what the Dean is saying works and your cannons succeed in defeating the Merchant's fleet, you would lose the gold forever. Venus' belly is not made of wood like the rest of the ships. It is made of steel.'

The Red King leant in close. 'Steel?'

'Yes, your Grace, steel. The belly is made from a steel chamber that, if submerged, the water pressure turns a lock to which only the Merchant has the key. No one knows where he keeps the key or what it looks like. If the belly is locked underwater, we cannot pull it out. The gold will stay in there forever.' The First Man stood and glared at the Dean. 'I know the fleet, the men, and their code and protocol. I know how to get you the gold because I ...' He patted his chest. 'I am the First Man.'

Chapter 42

The sailor surveyed his surroundings. *The lighthouse ... always a place of fascination,* he thought to himself. The sailor smiled as he realised he had never been in a lighthouse before, having seen numerous but never entering any. *What a first.* He tapped his bowl with his spoon. "Thank you for the soup. It was delicious."

The old keeper didn't reply and continued sipping his soup rhythmically. The sailor sat back and watched the rain, whipped up by the wind, smashing against the window.

When the old keeper finished his soup, he set the plate aside, rubbed his mouth with a cloth, and held up a finger. "I forgot!" He slapped his forehead with his hand. "I knew that I had forgotten a part."

"What's that?" the sailor asked.

"I forgot a part of the story."

"What part?"

"Pale Face ..." The sailor nodded, and the old keeper continued. "After the head gunner passed away, the Merchant tested each gunner in his crew, but no one was up to the standard. See, Venus' fire force was fierce and heavy to handle. Not just because it had many fire floors and cannons, it was ... tricky ... the mechanism was unique and confusing."

"How?" the sailor asked.

"The cannons were connected. Every four cannons were attached and loaded and fired all together at the same time.

They were retracted, ejected, or switched from starboard to port sides by a hand leveller. So, the head gunner had to memorise the fire pattern of all fire floors, synchronise them, and cue the firing, especially since not all the cannons on Venus had the same range."

The sailor raised his eyebrows. "Oh boy, that does sound confusing. But how would the main gunner communicate with all fire floors?"

"Through copper tubes. He shouted his commands into a tube, and each floor had a listener who shouted the command repeatedly to the fire crew. The head gunner had a control spot on the top fire floor with all the copper tubes and levellers. That's why they all called him top gunner. After the Merchant tested all the gunners, he couldn't find a fitting replacement until he tested one man." The old keeper wagged a finger. "Not from the crew, but from shore. A man who was on a ship he had rescued from pirates, a man who was on the captain's ship when it was attacked but never sailed back with it. He stayed in the Silver harbour. Pale Face."

Chapter 43

The sailor listened intently as the old keeper continued. "After recruiting Pale Face, leaving the First Man behind, and digging the swords in the Silvers' shore, the Merchant sailed back to the kingdom of World's Edge, where his beloved Isabella was preparing for their wedding.

After the wedding, for the first time, the Merchant docked his fleet for a month and took Isabella to a hidden tropical island where they ate nothing but fruits and honey. Their love for each other was manifested in dance, touch, hugs and kisses. Away from everyone, they were free to enjoy each other and only each other. They were blissfully happy because they had all they had ever wanted or needed – the love of each other.

But the moon was darker on the other side. While the Merchant was gone for months, the Dean, the Minister, the Red King, and the First Man laid a carefully plotted plan to bring the Merchant down. Every time the First Man had hesitated, his beloved Prima had persuaded him to continue. So, eventually, he had given them every detail they needed, every weakness, every flaw, every secret. To him, it was all about winning Prima – that is what assuaged his conscience and warmed his heart. Winning Prima was all there was, and nothing else mattered. Not even the Merchant."

Chapter 44

Crowned queen of the Merchant's fleet, Isabella hardly removed her tiara. The months she spent aboard were the happiest she had ever been. She was finally with the one she loved. She knew him and truly understood the Merchant as no other did. She held his secrets, his heart, and over time her feelings had deepened further into a boundless and all-consuming love for him.

After a long journey back to the Red and Silver Kingdoms, the Merchant's fleet finally reached the Silver port. After skipping greeting the Red King on his last visit, the Merchant was determined to see the Red King first – out of courtesy.

The Red Kingdom's guards lined up and received the Merchant on the beach before announcing his arrival, 'The Merchant!' the voices rang out. But the Merchant was unhappy with this and asked the guards to repeat the announcement, proclaiming that his queen, Isabella, was there too.

The guards, at first hesitant, eventually acceded to his request. 'The Merchant …' the Red guards shouted, 'the Merchant and … his queen!'

Back at the Red Castle, the Queen jumped from her seat, furious at what she had heard. 'What? I am the Queen. I am the only Queen,' she screamed.

'Welcome, my dear friend,' the Red King said to the Merchant as he entered the royal hall with Isabella holding his hand. 'Ah … so this is the beautiful Queen Isabella I have heard so much about.' The Red King appraised her and smiled before stepping forward and offering his hand. 'Congratulations,' he said. 'May you have all the happiness in the world. And of course …' He looked at the Merchant, '… whoever has the Merchant has the world, am I right?' The Red King laughed, then turned back to his throne. 'Tonight, my friends, we celebrate. The Red Castle will rejoice in this momentous occasion. You're invited to a royal banquet in celebration of your marriage.'

'Thank you, your Highness,' the Merchant said.

'I hope your marriage lasts eternally. For there is no greater loss than to lose the one we love.' The Red King sighed, briefly lowered his head and then smiled. 'Go back to your ship, rest, and I'll see you tonight.'

'We will rest shortly, but we have gifts, your Highness. My men are—'

The Red King slumped onto his throne. 'No! Today I shall receive no presents from you. I will not accept your present tonight.' He waved a hand at one of his guards. 'I will give you my present instead. My guards will fetch it for you.'

'Thank you for such generosity, your Highness.' The Merchant nodded, and holding on tightly to Isabella's hand, they left. The Red King scowled as he watched them leave.

Chapter 45

After greeting the Red King, the Merchant and Isabella travelled to the Silver Kingdom to greet the Silver King before returning to the ship. His greetings this time were short and brief. Clearly, the Merchant was eager to spend more time with Isabella alone.

The First Man waited for the Merchant aboard Venus and rushed to him as soon as he arrived onboard.

'Welcome back,' the First Man greeted the Merchant.

'Thank you,' the Merchant said, glancing at Isabella and then back to the First Man again.

The First Man bowed his head at Isabella. 'Welcome back, and congratulations. I heard that the wedding was exquisite.'

Isabella smiled. 'Thank you very much. It was.'

The Merchant narrowed his eyes. 'Is everything ok? You seem … different!'

'No, not at all … everything is fine.' He shuffled his feet. 'I wanted to tell you that the Mute has been cured, and the spears and arrows are buried in the sand as you instructed, Merchant.' He forced a smile.

'Ok,' the Merchant said, nodding. He and Isabella turned and headed to the house, but after walking a few steps away, the Merchant stopped and looked back at the First Man. 'Are you sure you are ok?'

'Yes! Yes, I am,' The First Man said.

The Merchant glanced at him, then headed off with his wife.

Chapter 46

That night, at the Red Castle, a lavish dinner was prepared and laid out on an enormous table in the centre of the Red Castle's royal hall. Music played, dancers swirled, and a variety of entertainers left no space for boredom. It was an exquisite royal dinner banquet. The Red King sat at the head of the table with the Queen opposite him on the other end. The Merchant and Isabella sat beside each other in the middle of the table, on the Red King's right and the Queen's left.

'Help yourself to more food,' the Red King said to Isabella.

'Thank you, your Highness, but I am full.' She dabbed at her lips with a napkin. 'That is quite a feast, if I may say so,' Isabella said, setting her plate aside.

The Queen, who had been quiet all night, stared down and prodded at her barely eaten food as she pushed it around the plate. The Red King, of course, showed no concern. On the contrary, he was overly friendly. 'Then let's have a drink to mark the occasion,' the Red King said, signalling the servant to pour wine for the Merchant and Isabella.

The Merchant placed his hand over the empty glass to his side. 'Pardon me, Red King, but you know I don't drink.'

The Red King threw his head back and roared with laughter. 'Well, this is something I always wondered about. How could a sailor not drink? Don't you add wine to your water to keep it fresh? Wine prevents it from going bad during months in the middle of the sea, am I right?'

'Yes, you are right. Wine does keep the water fresh, but so does silver. We use pure silver coins to keep our water and minds fresh.'

'Ah, an answer to every question and a new trick to every old way. No wonder everyone I know is fascinated by you,' the Red King slurred. 'May I ask you, and I have never asked anything of you before, but would you have a drink with me tonight? After all, this is one occasion to celebrate.'

The Merchant studied the King briefly, then nodded for one of the servants to fill his glass. He glanced at Isabella and then drank the wine.

The Red King smiled and sat back in his chair. 'Tell us, Isabella, how did you both meet? I bet it is an interesting story.' He leant forward. 'Come on, tell us, don't be shy.'

'I have nothing to be shy of, your Highness,' Isabella said. 'I will gladly tell you how we met.' She took hold of the Merchant's hand and smiled at her husband, who gently squeezed hers. Her eyes sparkled, and she took a deep breath and began. 'I was walking in the woods, at dusk, on my way home,' Isabella said.

'She was wearing a red hood, carrying a breadbasket in her right hand,' the Merchant said.

Isabella continued, 'It got dark, then I heard crackling behind me, so I hurried towards the cottage. I was scared, and the sound appeared to be getting nearer. No matter how I quickened my step, it was still closing on me.'

The Queen rolled her eyes and sipped at her drink. 'What was it?'

'Let her finish the story. Their story,' the Red King said and smiled at Isabella. 'Please, go on,' he said.

'As I said, I was afraid, it was dark, and the sound of something moving in the woods was catching up, so I started running. All I thought about was that I wanted to get home and be safe. I wasn't even curious to know what was making that sound. Anything or anyone following me in the woods at that time is something I'd rather not face. I ran and ran, and still it got closer and louder. I foolishly looked behind, tripped and fell, and as I looked up, it stood over me. The biggest wolf I had ever seen. Its eyes bore down on me as if looking into my soul. With steaming breath and razor-like teeth, I thought that was it. I screamed, but before the wolf attacked, someone leapt from the trees at lightning speed and, face to face with the wolf, with a dagger in each hand, he confronted it. Before I knew it, they were locked in battle. He with his daggers, the wolf with those horrid teeth, until, finally, after what seemed an eternity, the man managed to climb onto the Beast's back and stab it with his blades. Blood spurted from the animal, and it let out an ear-piercing howl as it slumped onto the floor with both knives embedded deeply into its neck. The Merchant stood before me.' Isabella smiled at her husband again.

'She stayed on the ground,' the Merchant said. 'She was so scared, I lent her my hand, but it took her a moment before she allowed me to help her up.'

'He seemed so fearless that I feared him myself,' Isabella said. 'I remember our conversation that night as he walked me home. His bravery overwhelmed me, so I asked him what he feared the most. I still remember the answer so clearly.'

'So, what does the Merchant fear the most?' the Red King said. 'That is such an interesting question. What does a man who travels the world and conquers all seas fear? What do you fear the most, Merchant?'

Isabella leant in closer. 'He told me that the only thing he feared was—'

The Merchant placed a hand on his wife's arm. 'Myself,' he said. 'I fear myself the most ... your Highness ... I fear myself the most.' The Merchant rubbed his eyes as his vision blurred.

The Red King laughed. 'Don't tell me that one cup of wine got to you, Merchant.'

'Are you all right?' Isabella asked.

'Yes, dear, don't worry, I am fine,' the Merchant said, gently squeezing her hand.

The Red King stood. 'So then, before the night comes to an early end, may I give you my present?' He began to circle the table. 'To be honest ... and humble ... it was a hard one.

Difficult even for a king.' He paused his walking and then continued again. 'What would I get the Merchant as a wedding gift? After all, he already has or can have anything he wants from any place around the world. How can I impress the Merchant with a single present, I thought to myself.' The King put a finger in the air. 'Then it occurred to me that it must be artistic – art is the finest gift of all. I am a writer. I write poetry that no one knows about. Words are the best gift I can give you.'

The Merchant struggled to focus on the King as his vision blurred further. He reached for his water and drank greedily. The Red King, ignoring his guest, continued, 'So, I searched and searched my poems and lucky enough, I came across a better writer than myself. A writer who falls short of none when it comes to the expression of the emotions of love and passion. A wonderful poem.' He narrowed his eyes at the Merchant and Isabella. 'Unfortunately, the writer didn't give a name to the piece, so I gave it a title myself. I called it Ink & Blood.' The Red King growled as he pulled the Queen's crumpled love letter from his pocket to the Merchant and threw it into the middle of the table. The Merchant immediately recognised the letter, identical to the ones he had returned to her. The Queen's mouth dropped open as she stared at the paper. The Merchant, now panting, mopped his sweaty brow with his napkin. He was sure it wasn't just the wine making him feel ill. He looked to the Red King and then at his empty wine glass as realisation dawned. There was something in his drink, in revenge for the Queen's love for him.

'What is going on?' Isabella said as she held onto her swaying husband. 'What is happening to you?' She shook his arm, but the Merchant could hardly speak.

'Guards,' the Red King shouted. The music stopped, and the guests and servants hurried from the hall. Royal guards surrounded Isabella and pulled the Merchant to his feet, dragging him towards the King. The Merchant looked up through bleary eyes, his legs unable to support him, as the royal guards held him upright in front of their monarch. The Red King stepped nearer and grabbed the Merchant pulling him closer.

'We are almost even,' the Red King said to the Merchant. 'You captured my queen's heart, but I have captured your Isabella.'

'I … I … I never … loved her back,' the Merchant said with short breaths. 'I gave her no encouragement.'

The King sneered. 'Oh, Merchant. Does it really matter?' The Red King drew his dagger and thrust it into the Merchant's stomach. Isabella cried out as the Queen gasped. 'No!' Isabella said, getting to her feet, but the Red guards held her back. The Red King, still holding onto the blade, lowered his head towards the Merchant. 'Go back to your fleet, order them to surrender without a fight. If a single cannon is fired at this castle, you'll never see Isabella again. I will slit her throat myself with this very dagger.' He withdrew the blade slowly, and the Merchant grimaced and fell to the floor. The Red guards seized Isabella and dragged her from the royal hall as the Queen fled to her chamber. The Merchant looked up at the smirking Red King and attempted to climb onto one knee. He pulled a handkerchief from his pocket and pushed it against his wound as his attacker looked on.

The Red King grabbed the shoulder of his victim and shook him. 'She was my world, and you stole her from me. Give me your fleet in return. Give me the world.'

The Merchant groaned and pushed the King's hand away. 'No!'

The Red King roared and kicked the Merchant, catching him on the side of his head. The Merchant fell backwards, and the King drew his sword and began hitting the stricken Merchant repeatedly.

The door burst open, and the First Man stormed in, ran across to the pair, grabbed the King's arm and halted the attack. 'What are you doing?' the First Man said. 'If he dies here, they will raise your castle to the ground. We agreed you would only wound him.'

The Red King stepped backwards and slumped to the floor, breathing heavily. He tossed aside his weapon and wept. The Merchant, lying on his side, opened an eye and briefly looked at his First Man before consciousness failed him.

Chapter 47

The First Man took the wounded Merchant back to the ship. He explained to the crew how the Red King had gone mad, wounded the Merchant, and kept Isabella prisoner until the fleet surrendered. The First Man told them everything, not out of honesty, but instead, he acted according to the plan.

When the Silvers heard about the incident, they sent their naval commander to Venus that night. The naval commander visited the Merchant, who lay bleeding and unconscious. Despite the healers' efforts to treat and dress the wounds and using every medicine at his disposal, he could not stop the bleeding. The treatment slowed the loss of blood but didn't stop it. As much as the Silvers' naval commander was concerned about the Merchant's well-being, he was also worried about what would happen next. If the Red King got hold of the Merchant's fleet, it only meant one thing to the Silvers – a wipe-out of the Silver fleet and, later, the whole Silver Kingdom.

'How is he doing?' the naval commander asked the First Man.

'He is still unconscious,' the First Man said. 'I have treated his wounds as best as I can, but the bleeding will not cease.'

The naval commander frowned as he looked at the stricken Merchant. 'I will assemble our fighting ships and join your fleet to enforce against any possible attacks.'

'The Merchant's men can defend the fleet,' the First Man said.

'But the Merchant is wounded. Your men are concerned about their leader and will not fight with high morale. You need us … and we must defend the Merchant's fleet.'

'You would be stepping into the Red Kingdom's waters.' the First Man said.

'Yes, I realise that.'

'That would enrage the Red King further and make matters worse,' the First Man said.

The naval commander glanced at the Merchant again. 'I don't think things could be worse..' He nodded at the First Man and returned to his commanding ship.

The First Man smiled, knowing that all he had to do was wait because everything was going according to plan – his well-laid plan.

Chapter 48

The Red King stood by the narrow window, silently gazing outside until dawn. He was distant, leaning one hand on the wall above his head while the other clenched the wrinkled love letter. The Minister entered and hurried across to him. 'Sire,' he said through captured breaths. The Red King continued to stare into the distance. The Minister edged closer. 'Your Highness … Sire … my king.'

The Red King turned to face his Minister.

'I was wondering if the guards should—' the Minister said.

'Keep your chin up,' the Red King whispered.

'My king?'

'Keep your chin up, my father told me,' the Red King said. 'Keep your chin up, his father told him. Keep your chin up, for a crown only falls from a lowered head.' The Red King turned and gazed outside again.

The Minister furrowed his brow. 'Sire?'

The Red King spun around and glowered at his Minister. 'Declare Royal Anger.'

'But …?' the Minister stammered.

'Declare, Royal, Anger,' the Red King stressed every word.

'Sire … Royal Anger is just … it has never been …'

The Red King stepped forward, grabbed the Minister, and pushed him backwards. 'Do not contradict me. I said declare Royal Anger.' He lowered his eyes at the cowering Minister. 'Declare Royal Anger and condemn the Queen.' The Minister gasped and wiped his tear-filled eyes. 'Your Highness, Prima, my only daughter … pardon her … let her go home before you declare …'

The Red King turned and stood with his hands behind his back. 'I … King of the Red Kingdom …'

'No!' the Minister pleaded.

'… Declare Royal Anger upon the Red Marbled Castle!'

'No! Your Highness, I beg you … pardon Prima. Pardon my daughter!'

The Red King continued, 'In condemnation of the Queen and all her subjects.' He crumpled the Queen's love letter to the Merchant and threw it aside. 'Guards,' he shouted. The royal guards appeared and knelt before him. 'You may announce Royal Anger.'

The royal guards banged their spears loudly on the ground, repeating the Red King's declaration. One after the other, throughout the castle, from the centre throne hall to the deepest hollow below, the order was exclaimed.

The Minister knew what it meant, and, pulling out his dagger, he lunged for the King. But the royal guards were quicker, and before the Minister could reach the monarch, they cut him down with their spears. The Red King turned and looked down at the blood-covered Minister as his life ebbed away. The King stood tall and puffed out his chest as the Red Castle echoed to the sound of his guards.

'Royal Anger! … Royal Anger! … Royal Anger!' they proclaimed.

Chapter 49

The Silvers assembled their fleet into several units – most of which were commanded to join and reinforce the Merchant's fleet. Two of them headed north. These were stationed to give an early alarm and defend the northern front of the Silver Kingdom.

As soon as they dropped anchor, men atop the main tower scanned the horizon with their telescopes, a routine they were well trained for. Starting from the east side, they slowly panned west, then back to the middle of the horizon, to the furthest point north. One after another, they all flawlessly performed the task.

One of the men paused as he looked deep into the northern horizon. He put down his telescope, checked the horizon with his eyes, and then looked back through the telescope – now certain of what he had seen. A fleet, a whole fleet of pirate ships. Dozens of them filled his field of vision as if every pirate ship from all the seas were heading towards them.

Chapter 50

Cannons on top of the Red Castle repeatedly fired, filling the air with thick, black smoke. The flags around the castle were dropped to half mast, and in the centre, an enormous black flag was raised on a huge pole. As a cloud of black billowed above the castle and across the bay, the cannons relentlessly continued their barrage.

Deep down in the belly of the castle, doors to the dungeons were flung open. Dungeons that held inside the Royal Anger executors. These men, known for their lethal force, were tall, broad, tough African men. They had lived and trained in the dungeons every day and night for years, never truly believing they would ever be needed. The role of Royal Anger executor was considered a ceremonial position, for Royal Anger had never been implemented – the idea of its existence being symbolic and strategic. But on that day, the dungeons were opened, and masked, muscular men dressed in black leather were ordered to execute their task, and they knew precisely what to do. Though rarely spoken of up above, the mere mention of their names could terrify the castle's inhabitants and surrounding area. They were called the Slayers.

Chapter 51

The First Man stood onboard Venus, leaning against the port side. The Silver naval commander stood next to him, and together they gazed at the giant cloud of black smoke surrounding the Red Castle.

'What's that?' the First Man said, squinting.

The naval commander frowned and slowly shook his head. 'That is something I had heard about but thought and hoped I would never witness.' He briefly closed his eyes. 'It can't be,' he mumbled.

The First Man took hold of his arm. 'What does it mean?'

'It means that the Red King is angry to the extent that he's lost his mind. Anger has driven him insane. The Red King is angry like no other king has ever been …' The naval commander turned sharply to the north as horns echoed across the horizon.

'What now?' the First Man asked.

The naval commander turned to him. 'Gather your ships and follow mine. The battle has begun.'

Chapter 52

A group of fair-haired girls wearing white silk dresses ran through the halls of the Red Castle. Each one held a bucket full of black paint so thick it resembled tar. They swiftly spread out and began daubing the portraits hung on the walls – obliterating any containing the Queen's face. Even group paintings were not spared the onslaught. One after another brutally defaced, leaving the pictures and walls covered in the black, viscous liquid dripping from them like black teardrops – the tears of Royal Anger.

The Slayers sought out the Queen's guards, slaughtering them mercilessly before dismembering their bloodied corpses. Screams of pain and panic resounded throughout the castle. Although the guards resisted, they were powerless against the Slayers as, one by one, they succumbed.

The girls swept into the Red King's throne hall and painted the King's throne black. Then, wheeling in a giant crystal heart full of black paint, they handed the Red King a small black metal hammer. The Red King broke the heart, set the hammer aside, dipped his hand into the paint, and took out a key.

One of the girls took the key from him, ran to a black wooden door, and unlocked it. Behind the door lay a crown, seal rings, a sceptre, and a robe, all of which were a replica of the king's royal belongings – an exact copy, but for one thing, they were all black.

Removing the Red King's crown, they replaced it with its replica. Then they took off his robe, laid the black one on his shoulders, and handed him the black sceptre. The Red King remained expressionless throughout the process, his hand still clutching the Queen's love letter to the Merchant.

The screams from the Queen's guards outside her chamber door were terrifying. As her maids huddled together, shaking on the floor, they listened to the screaming outside. The Queen sat on her throne, dressed in white and wearing her crown. The silence that followed frightened them more than the noises from outside.

The Queen knew that the Slayers had killed her guards. The maids screamed louder and held on to each other as the door banged and rattled.

The Slayers were tearing her chamber door down. With every bang, the Queen trembled more, and the maid's screams intensified as they held on tighter to each other.

Finally, the door shattered and fell to the floor as the Slayers stepped inside.

At the front stood the largest and most-powerful Slayer. He slowly walked towards the Queen. She met his gaze, and trying desperately to control her trembling, she stared at him. He sneered and knocked the crown from her head.

The fair girls entered and positioned themselves next to the Queen's bathtub. Then, lifting the paint buckets onto their shoulders, they stood still.

The head Slayer pointed to the bathtub, and the Queen, with her head lifted high, made her way towards it. As she passed by her maids, she gently slid her hand across their heads, touching each in turn. They cried out in anger and pain as the Queen's eyes filled with tears. She reached the bath and stood at the top of the steps leading to it. She glanced at her maids and the creamy white water, then lifted her chin and looked at the Slayer.

The Slayer nodded to the girls, who poured the black paint from their buckets over the Queen, and as she descended the steps into the water, it turned from white to black.

The Queen dipped into the water and watched as her maids were taken by the Slayers. The tears she had managed to hold onto for so long finally cascaded down her face. She closed her eyes and lifted her chin defiantly as the girls continued to empty their buckets over her. Eventually, they finished, and covered from head to toe, she stood and stepped from the bath. The Slayer growled and motioned for her to hold out her hands. Handcuffs snapped shut around her wrists, a chain was attached to these, and then she was pulled barefoot through the halls past bodies covered in blood. She averted her eyes but couldn't help looking at the people she had lived with, who had looked after and kept her safe, lying slaughtered all around her. Her knees grew weaker as they approached the Red King's throne hall, a thick trail of black followed her as she struggled to remain upright. The Slayer opened the door and pulled her across the floor. She stood alone, a pitiful sight, in front of the Red King and his Royal Anger.

Chapter 53

The Red King sat on his black-painted throne as the Queen eyed a portrait hanging on the wall – her face obliterated and daubed in black. The Red King held up her love letter to the Merchant and narrowed his eyes at her. 'Why?' he said. The Queen lowered her head but said nothing.

'Why?' the Red King shouted, throwing the letter at her. The Queen remained silent, and the Red King jumped from his throne and strode across to her. He grabbed her arm and roughly shook her. 'Why? Tell me why?' Tears dropped from his eyes as he released her. 'What have I done to deserve this? After all I've done … this …' He picked up the letter and pushed it into her face. 'This is how you pay me back?'

The Queen lifted her head and sneered. 'Pay you back? That's an interesting use of words. Is it because you think you paid me somehow? And what did you pay for?' She stared at him. 'Did you think you could buy me with all the pearls, silk and jewels you've given me? And you expected me to pay you back? Well, all efforts to buy me didn't work.'

'Buy you!' the Red King said.

'Yes … you thought you could—'

'Buy you?' the Red King said and frowned.

'Why are you—' she said.

'Buy you! Buy you!' The Red King moved across to his throne and threw open a chest next to it. He pulled out a pearl necklace and held it up in front of the Queen's face. 'These reminded me of your smile, so I bought them for you.' He threw it down at the feet of the Queen and then pulled out a silk cloth. 'And this. This is how your skin felt to me, so I bought it for you.' The Red King allowed it to fall and drift towards the Queen. 'And these …' he said, scooping up a handful of jewels. 'All of these are not a fraction of how precious you are … you were … to me.' He opened his fingers, allowing them to fall from his hand, and then stared at the floor.

The Queen stood silent as the Red King lifted his head and looked her in the eye. 'A man does what he can to express his love, and you … you were loved by a king.' He opened his arms, palms upwards. 'I never tried to buy you. A king never buys his Queen. He wins her heart.'

She stepped forward and then stopped, gazing at her husband. His shoulders drooped, and his head lowered towards his chest. A lump appeared in her throat as she tried to speak, and tears ran down her cheek. Her words remained unsaid.

The Red King turned his back to her. 'Guards,' he shouted, 'take her to the dungeons.' The Queen moved forward again, but the guards gripped her arms tightly. The King remained motionless as only the clinking of the chains could be heard as she was dragged from the room. 'Take her away, now,' he shouted as they left.

Chapter 54

The First Man joined the Silver naval commander, merged with the other battleships, and sailing at top speed, they headed towards the pirate's fleet. The battle had to be won, and the pirates halted in the middle of the sea, or the damage would be severe. The Silver naval commander scanned the horizon as the First Man looked backwards at the Red Castle, gazing at the huge black cloud of smoke billowing over it. He was worried for Prima more than ever before.

What is going on in the Red Castle? he thought to himself. No one mentioned such a thing while we were planning all this, not the Minister, not the Red King, not even Prima.

He joined the Silver naval commander. 'I am just curious,' the First Man said, 'but what is happening on shore? The Red Castle, the black smoke and the black flags? What is that all about?'

'Later,' the Silver naval commander said. 'Draw your sword and be ready. We are getting close.'

The sound of cannons came into earshot as they neared the battle spot. As the noise increased in intensity, it was obvious that the battle was fierce.

'I think we should split up,' the First Man shouted as the sounds of the ongoing battle increased further.

'What? Split? Now? Why?' the naval commander asked as he fastened his belt and checked his sword.

'They outnumber us. We must distract their attack. You go

and support the remaining Silver ships. I will circle to draw their attention and find a weak spot. I can do them severe damage.'

The naval commander pondered this for a moment and frowned. He glanced towards the raging battle again as they came within distance of the enemy's cannons. 'Very well,' he said. 'Meet me in the middle.'

The First Man headed for his own ship.

The naval commander scrutinised the First Man and watched him leave.

About five hundred of the Merchant ships circled the battle spot and the First Man commanded them all. They were close to the pirates' fleet but not too close to get hit by cannon fire. The First Man turned to one of the officers. 'Signal them to line up,' he said. The officer nodded and passed on the order. This was repeated throughout the fleet until every ship had received it. The vessels followed. Each ship adjusted its speed until they all lined up sideways.

'The line is formed,' the First Man's second in command said.

'Then fire,' the First Man ordered.

'Fire!' The ships fired their cannons. The Merchant's fleet was famous for its powerful long-range cannons and one pirate ship after another was hit repeatedly until it was shattered into pieces.

The second in command looked on bemused. After the first couple of shots, the pirate ships never fired back. They just waited like sitting ducks while the Merchant's fleet destroyed them. 'Why aren't they firing back?'

The First Man smirked. 'Why would they?'

'I know we are out of their range, but still, they didn't even try to get close …' He grimaced and clutched his stomach. He began to sweat and dropped onto one knee as the pain intensified and the colour faded from his face.

The First Man ignored him. 'They will get close.'

The second in command gathered his strength. Ignoring his rising nausea, he stood and viewed the debris through his telescope. 'There aren't any bodies?' he said, breathing heavily and struggling to maintain his balance.

'No, the ships were empty, or they abandoned the ships before we shot at them.'

The second in command dropped his telescope and holding onto the First Man's arm, he fell to his knees. He looked around at the rest of the crew vomiting, all except the First Man, who stood with his hands behind his back looking out to sea.

He looked at his superior. 'You've poisoned us. Why?'

'Why?' the First Man muttered. He sneered at his junior. 'Because I am in love with the most beautiful fairness I have ever seen, Prima. I'd do anything to be with her. I would lose it all to win her.' He grasped the arm of the stricken man. 'They say love makes a fool out of a man, but no, I am not fooling myself. I know what I've done. I have betrayed you all.' He smiled. 'I dropped the poisoned silver coins into the water tanks. Thirst is at its most right before battle. Two silver coins stuck together with poison that the Blacks gave me was enough for each tank. As soon as it dissolves, it disappears, leaving no colour, no smell, no taste and no chance of survival.' He laughed. 'It kills. It certainly kills. I've killed you all … for love gets the best out of a person … or the worst.'

'Throw the rope, don't leave us in the locker, throw us the rope,' the second in command pleaded, but the First Man stood still and watched him as slowly, painfully, he died.

The First Man took out of his pocket a black paper roll and set fire to it. Thick black smoke billowed from the burning paper, and the pirates' ships emerged just as planned from behind the shattered and burnt decoy ships. They boarded the Merchant's ships, put on the poisoned men's clothes, and then threw their bodies into the water. The First Man looked on passively. For now, he controlled half of the Merchant's fleet. All was going well. All was going according to plan.

'Love gets the best out of one, or the worst,' the First Man whispered. 'I betrayed them for your sake … my love.'

Chapter 55

The Mute ran back to his home. His mother was sweeping the dust in front of the house with a shorthanded broom. She turned as she spotted her son running toward the house, put down her brush, and dropped to her knees with open arms. The Mute threw himself into them, hugging her tightly.

'My sweetest, what's wrong?' She eased him away and cupped his face in her hands.

'He is hurt,' the Mute signed. 'Badly. He is wounded badly. Blood everywhere, the Merchant, the Merchant is badly wounded.' He put his head onto his mother's shoulder, and she patted him on the back as he sobbed. His twin brother stood a couple of steps away. She looked across and beckoned him to join her and his brother, and the three of them joined in a tearful embrace.

The mother had raised her two sons – born after their father's death. He was killed in a battle of no return far beyond the horizon. She remembered the day they were born so clearly, as if it was a week ago. A hard and lengthy labour. In pain, sweating, and screaming for what seemed an eternity. The horror of giving birth evaporated when she laid eyes on her firstborn. Then another child – her twins. Then another pain enveloped her. Not a physical one but an emotional one. A loneliness ached in her chest, clutched at her heart, and squeezed the tears from her eyes. Now alone, she would have to raise the boys on her own. She was afraid, sad, and anxious. Her despair was bottomless, and in her darkest hour, he arrived – the Merchant himself. He stepped into her poor house and pledged to care for the family. She smiled through her tears and thanked him. The Merchant, as always, kept his word, paid off her debts, and supported them with gold coins, clothes, medicines, and whatever else they needed, but most important of all, he taught the Mute how to speak sign language. She would never have been able to communicate with her dearest. She would never have truly known him or been able to express her love if it wasn't for the Merchant. And now, he lay, wounded, bleeding, and dying.

Chapter 56

The Silver naval commander was one of the greatest commanders of the Silver Kingdom, a master of numerous battles, but this time, somehow … it was different.

The pirates were fierce and confident, pulling in and out in a well-laid naval tactic. As they tightened their grip around his ships, he thought, 'Where are you?' Every word stressed in his mind as he wielded his sword with all his strength against the enemy overwhelming his ship.

The gun battle had been fierce – many of his fleet had been boarded, including his own, forcing him and his crew into a face-to-face sword fight.

He glimpsed the masts of the First Man's fleet nearby, strengthening his resolve to battle on. Relief flooded through him, knowing that five hundred ships of the Merchant's fleet were more than needed to win this battle.

Anytime now, the cannons would fire, and the pirates would sink, just as planned with the First Man. The guns fired, and smoke filled the air as the cannonade continued. The Silver naval commander almost smiled as he and his crew battled to overcome the marauding pirates. But then a realisation took hold. The cannons weren't firing at the pirate ships but at the Silver ships, sending them to the ocean floor like rocks dropped into a pool.

Dispirited by what he saw, he dropped his guard, and

something struck him hard across his chin. He stumbled backwards and fell as his consciousness failed him.

Chapter 57

The dense forest behind the Red Castle overlooked everything – the Red Castle, the Silver Castle, the Crab Gulf, and the Teardrop Isles – protecting the castle from their enemies.

But atop that hill and another tree line lay another forest. And within the tree line was an area devoid of trees giving any observer a perfect panoramic view. A black horse carriage stopped at that spot. It was the Black family's Dean.

Renowned for keeping a close eye on what makes or breaks the family's future, today, he had decided to see for himself rather than rely on reports. On this momentous day, he couldn't sit and wait for news. He had to be there to witness the execution of his well-laid plan.

This day would be the start of all days for him and his family. A new horizon. The Merchant, his fleet and his men would all perish along with The Red and Silver Kingdoms. They would burn in fires … fires that would herald and light the way for the Black family to rise.

Chapter 58

T he Silvers watched from the highest towers of their kingdom and witnessed it all. They saw the Merchant's men dying and being thrown into the waters. They saw the pirates dressing in the Merchant's men's clothes to disguise themselves. They saw the Silver naval commander and his men slaughtered and the pirates taking over the ships, but worst of all, they saw the First Man's betrayal. They had witnessed his darkness.

'They are heading to us,' one watcher said to the other.

'They will be here by night,' his companion said. 'Hurry to the commanders.'

'Shall I send someone to warn the Merchant's fleet, too?'

'The commanders will tell us what to do. Hurry to them, now!'

He rushed down the tower as ordered while the watcher returned to his telescope. The remainder of the Merchant's and Silver's fleet sat silently, still anchored in the Crab Gulf. The pirate vessels were heading towards the shore. 'They are going to attack tonight,' he muttered to himself.

Chapter 59

Horns blared in the Silver Kingdom. Horns that most villagers had never heard in their lives, but they all knew what it meant. Scared, crying, and panicking, the villagers lined up in front of their houses. They knew the drill – gather your family and loved ones, carry only your most essential belongings, and wait in front of your house.

The Silver guards came and led them out of the kingdom. The evacuation was not only to lead the people away from the enemy and the seaborne attack but also because the Reds had massed downhill. And this meant only one thing – they were mounting an offensive by land and sea. Something the Silver Kingdom had never before had to face.

Chapter 60

The Line guards were familiar to both the Red and Silver Kingdoms. These were the guards at the borderline that separated the two neighbouring realms. There was no forest between them, no river, sea, mountain, or any other of nature's borderlines.

The Silver Kingdom topped a hill, and the Red Kingdom the lowlands up to the borderline, midway between the top and bottom.

The Silver guards patrolled the gates and hill but never crossed the line separating the two kingdoms.

This line was heavily guarded by the Red Kingdom's Line guards, who were strong, fierce, and ready to fight at any moment. Highly disciplined and formidable in battle. Their weapons, shields and special armour were exceptional. Highly trained and skilled, they were led by the Saharan – a brutal, savage soldier, stronger, more skilled, more loyal and most faithful to the Red King.

They say that the Red King saved him when he found him dying of thirst in the middle of the desert – an Arabian desert the Red King travelled to on one of his expeditions. Saving the Saharan was a rare act of kindness from the Red King, or maybe an intelligent act by which he won himself a devoted, strong, and skilled soldier. Since then, the Saharan had defended the line and was always ready to attack the Red King's enemies anytime and at any cost.

The Saharan lined up with his soldiers and was joined by more troops until they had built up a frightening formation at the border. For the first time in their prolonged standoff, the Reds were about to attack the Silvers.

143

Chapter 61

The Mute, his twin and their mother finally reached the cave by nightfall and sat together. For decades the caves had offered sanctuary for the Silver Kingdom's people – a well-protected place that the old, sick, and young hid in with their mothers, sisters, and daughters. The place the people fled to during battles.

The young ones, who had never experienced war before, were terrified. Candles were dotted around the cave giving a small degree of light to the gloom. The Silver soldiers kept the sanctuary well-equipped and ready for such emergencies – food and blankets were plentiful as the people awaited news.

The Mute's mother lit individual candles and handed them out as the elders and children wrapped themselves up, seeking warmth and comfort. After the candles were lit and everyone held one, the Mute's mother started to sing a prayer, and they all joined her.

It was a moonless night, and easy for warships to hide on the horizon. So, the Silver ships, or rather the remaining half of the Silver fleet, stood in formation, a little offshore, waiting for their enemy to approach under the dark curtain of night.

Over the years, they learnt that defence of their kingdom instead of attacking the enemy was the best strategy on such nights. They waited, but no ships had shown up so far. It was a quiet and bitterly-cold evening. The waters calm and troubling, and the tension was palpable as they continued their wait.

Chapter 62

The Merchant lay in his bed, wounded, unconscious, and his breathing laboured. His worried men stood around him, sad, confused, and helpless. The situation appeared hopeless. The healers, unable to fully stem the blood loss, had dressed the cuts to his chest, stomach, and shoulders as best they could. But, despite this, the sheets he lay on were soaked with blood. Desperation filled the air as they hoped, prayed and waited for a miracle.

The chief healer sat on the edge of the bed, his eyes full of unshed tears and his heart filled with heaviness.

'Master,' he called gently, passing a small bottle under the Merchant's nose. 'Merchant … Merchant,' he called again, holding on desperately to his tears. But the Merchant remained unconscious.

At that moment, the door opened, the crowd parted, and Ji Kai strode inside. He approached the bed and stared down at the stricken Merchant. The healer stood and stepped aside. No one was sure if Ji Kai had come to bid farewell to his Master or save him. The assembled crowd watched on in silence.

Ji Kai pulled a small bottle from his pocket – its contents, a blue liquid, glowed in the dimly lit room. Opening the bottle, Ji Kai poured the glowing liquid into his wounds. He emptied the bottle and stood still while everyone around him waited. The Merchant inhaled a deep breath.

Ji Kai circled his hand over the Merchant's chest, and with

every move of Ji Kai's hand, the Merchant arched his back and inhaled deeply. His eyes were closed, but still, he responded to Ji Kai, and the Merchant lifted his back off the bed but then dropped back down, exhaling a long breath.

Seconds turned to minutes, yet the Merchant lay still. He did not inhale. He did not move. He did not breathe. At that moment, Ji Kai started to wave his hands in circles over the Merchant's head and body, mumbling words or sounds that no one understood but everyone felt. It was sad. It all sounded sad.

Ji Kai placed his arm under the Merchant's shoulders and knees, then surprisingly lifted him off the bed.

Despite his great age, he carried the Merchant out of the room. With heavy steps, the others followed him onto deck and across to the ship's port side, where a plank stretched out from the side over the water.

Walking along the length of the plank, Ji Kai stopped, closed his eyes, took a deep breath, briefly looked up to the sky, and then allowed the Merchant to roll from his arms, dropping him into the sea as the accustomed funeral practice.

The Merchant dropped like a rock to the seabed, leaving behind a cloudy trail of blood. Ji Kai tossed the end of a rope into the waters – the spirit rope – for the Merchant's spirit to climb back up to the ship. At that moment, they were all sure that the Merchant was gone.

Ji Kai chanted in some unusual language over and over. The wind picked up, lightning and thunder struck as rain cascaded from the heavens. Ji Kai pulled more blue bottles from his pocket and dropped them into the water. The water bubbled rapidly, as if boiling, and sharks circled the spot, driven towards the vessel by the Merchant's blood. Ji Kai chanted louder, the waters roiled, and the winds blew stronger, buffeting the ship, which strained against its moorings.

Suddenly, the loose rope tightened, and everybody stared, trying to decipher what was pulling it. Then, a hand stretched out of the water and, holding onto the rope, climbed up. It was the Merchant. He pulled himself free of the rumbling waters and circling sharks. As the thunder struck louder, he hauled himself back onto the ship. His ship.

He stood, panting from his exertions, in front of Ji Kai. His veins pumped up, and his wounds filled and sealed with the glowing blue liquid. His eyes were sharp and focused. Ji Kai continued his enchantments, dipped his thumb into more of the glowing blue liquid, and marked the Merchant's forehead with it.

The Merchant pushed through his cheering men, ran to the main mast, and rapidly climbed to the top. When his men saw this, they ran to their ships and climbed the masts.

When the Merchant reached the top, he grabbed a red horn and blew loudly. Each ship, in turn, did likewise until every vessel had sounded their horns. Pale Face loaded the three biggest cannons with as much gun-powder as they could take – only gunpowder, no cannon balls –and fired one after another. They were so loud that the battlements and ramparts on the castle shook, sending shockwaves down to the dungeon where the Queen sat trembling.

The Red King drew his sword on hearing the first shot and was shaken by the second. Still high up the mast, the Merchant roared as Pale Face fired the third shot. Everyone heard the shots, and they knew what it meant. The Merchant had returned and was ready to fight.

Chapter 63

The First Man listened intently as the sound of the horns and cannons could be clearly heard. After the third boom, he turned to the crew. 'Stop here!' he commanded. 'Drop the anchors.'

'Why?' one of the pirates asked.

'Haven't you heard the horns and cannons?' He glared at the pirate. 'The Merchant is back. He was almost dead, but now he is back.'

The pirate shrugged. 'So?'

The First Man growled. 'So! Aren't you aware of whom we are dealing with, of whom we have rivalled? You might think it is all about the ships and the fleet, but trust me, I was his right hand and First Man. None of you would want to face the Merchant now. We anchor here tonight and wait.' The First Man turned and looked towards where the sound had come from.

'Wait for what?'

The First Man glared at the pirate. 'For the Merchant to attack the Red King.'

Chapter 64

As dawn broke, it was cold, silent, and misty. The Red soldiers lined up on shore in full armour, spears pointing seaward. They stood motionless and ready, their eyes fixed on Venus.

The Merchant sat on the edge of his bed, gazing out the window into the pale first light of day. He picked up a little crystal bottle full of the blue liquid, opened it, and rubbed it on his head and body.

The Merchant's crew had changed from their everyday attire into their war costume. Everyone aboard Venus did this – sailors, cooks, and healers. Their outfits of gold, white and red gleamed beneath the rising sun. They were fighters now. Warriors and defenders of the Merchant, Venus, and his fleet. They lined up aboard their ships.

A large cymbal – a tam-tam gong – was placed atop the Merchant's house. The fleet's gong master stepped forward and struck the gong with a wrapped mallet. A terrifying sound rose to the sky and resonated outwards across the bay. The Red soldiers had never heard anything like it before, but it sounded like thunder. They lowered their spears, pointing them towards the Merchant's fleet and waited.

The Merchant left his house and stood before his men as drums beat out.

All eyes were on Venus. The Reds, Silvers, Blacks, pirates, and those behind the castle wall peeped through narrow windows.

The Merchant's men lowered a small boat into the water, and the Merchant descended a rope to it. He pointed inland, and the six crew onboard commenced rowing towards the shore. The Merchant stood at the bow with his eyes focused on the Red Castle, his eyes fixed on its battlements.

The Red soldiers started mumbling amongst themselves. The Merchant was nearing, and the Red King hadn't been able to kill him. His wounds had healed. He was strong and angry and coming their way. They glanced between themselves as the Beasts, down in the dungeons, roared. The noise rose to a crescendo as the Merchant neared.

The Red King watched from behind a narrow window in the throne hall, and as the Merchant approached the shore, he turned to his guards. 'Get Isabella here now!'

The Merchant stepped from the boat as his men stood up to their knees in the water and steadied the small craft. He looked up at the Red Castle's windows and narrowed his eyes. Isabella could be anywhere inside. Reliving the moment Isabella was taken from him, he roared and strode alone into the Red Castle.

For the first time, the Merchant walked through the hallows of the Red Castle unannounced. Royal Anger's protocol didn't welcome anyone.

The royal guards backed away from the Merchant and stood against the walls allowing him to pass through. He reached the throne hall, and the doors opened slowly. The Merchant stepped inside and surveyed the room. The Red King stood next to his black throne, and at the furthest corner stood Isabella, gripped tightly by a guard who held a blade to her neck.

The Merchant took a small black wooden box from his pocket and threw it on the floor in front of the Red King.

'Is this the key?' the Red King said as he scooped up the box and stared at the Merchant.

'Yes,' the Merchant said through gritted teeth.

The Red King frowned and turned the box around in his hands, trying to figure out how to open it. It seemed to be a solid piece of wood. 'How does it open?' he said.

'Burn it.'

The Red King scoffed. 'What?'

The Merchant glanced at Isabella, who smiled back. 'The box is a solid piece of wood,' he said. 'but the key is inside it, and it is metal. Burn the box, and recover the key from the ashes.'

The Red King smirked. 'The more precious the savings are, the trickier the safe gets.' He snapped his fingers. A guard plucked a torch from the wall and handed it to the Red King.

Slowly and carefully, the Red King offered the corner of the wooden box to the flame. The tip caught fire quickly but smouldered as a thin thread of black smoke drifted upwards. 'How can I be sure that what is inside is the actual key?'

'It changes colour in the rain,' the Merchant said. 'It turns from sky blue to purple if exposed to raindrops.'

The Red King pointed out of the window. 'It is not raining, and none is forecast. I must be sure that you haven't tricked me. If I sank Venus but could not get the gold ...' He studied the Merchant. 'You will have to stay here. You and her.' He nodded towards Isabella. 'You will remain here in the Red Castle, down in the dungeons, until I can drown that bloody ship and open the safe.'

The fire started to burn through the wooden box rapidly as the smoke got thicker. The Red King threw it onto the floor, and the smouldering box exploded.

The thick black smoke filled the hall, and everyone fell to the ground. Noise from outside could be heard through the windows as the sound of sword against sword drifted upwards. Everyone but the Merchant began coughing. He swiftly dispatched the guards standing beside him by breaking their necks. The guards outside the throne hall were reluctant to enter. The Merchant searched for Isabella, and spotting her through the acrid smoke, he ran to her. She dropped to her knees, coughing hard. The Merchant took a bottle from his jacket and allowed a few drops of the liquid to drip into her mouth. Isabella stopped coughing and looked up at her husband, who scooped her into his arms.

Thick black smoke billowed from the throne room's narrow window, and Pale Face directed Venus' cannons towards it.

The Merchant searched in the gloom, his eyes drawn to the Red King and guards on the floor, coughing and convulsing. He turned sharply as Red guards poured into the throne hall. Still carrying Isabella, he moved into the furthermost corner as Venus sent a cannonball crashing into the throne hall's outer wall, tearing a massive hole into it. The Merchant, clutching Isabella tightly, clambered over the rubble and through the Red Castle's shattered wall.

Chapter 65

The Saharan found it an excellent opportunity to use the assault on the castle and advance uphill to attack the Silvers.

'Follow me,' he said to his troops, and they swiftly crossed the line.

The Saharan knew that the distraction would only last briefly. He and his troops made their way upwards, attempting to reach the Silvers' troops before they realised what was happening, but the Silver Arch Knight, who had been keeping a watchful eye for such an incursion, spotted them. 'Attack!' he shouted, alerting his commanders to the advancing enemy.

Bows and spears rained down on the Saharan and his Line guards as the Silver troops mounted a fierce defence. The Saharan, however, used the terrain to his advantage, taking cover behind the rocks that littered the hillside. As soon as the Silver archers stopped to reload, the Saharan led his troops further up the slope, only stopping again when the wave of arrows and spears rained down. He was advancing slowly, but he was advancing smartly and steadily.

Chapter 66

The Red guards circled the Merchant and Isabella as soon as they emerged from the castle. Behind the Red guards, the Merchant could see three of the six men, who had accompanied him, lay dead while the other three fought fiercely against an overwhelming number of Red guards.

The cannons from the Merchant's vessels were silent as continuing the bombardment would have killed their own men as well as the Reds. It was a man-to-man fight, and the Merchant and his men were outnumbered as Isabella hid behind his back, shaking and crying.

But then the Red guards stopped and stepped back. The Merchant followed the Red soldier's gaze behind him. Isabella screamed and clutched her husband tighter.

The Merchant turned and was confronted by the two Beasts stepping from behind the rubble. Clearly, the cannon fire which had destroyed the walls had allowed them to escape.

The Red guards froze, but the Merchant didn't. He stepped closer to the Beasts while Isabella cowered behind him. The Beasts slowly circled the Merchant, sizing up the prey with razor-sharp teeth bared. They stepped closer to the Merchant and sniffed as their fur secreted the same blue liquid beneath their skin. Some of the braver Red guards edged closer, intending to mount a surprise attack against the Beasts so they could kill the Merchant. But the Beasts, as if sensing what they were trying to do, turned and roared, sending the guards scurrying away. One of the Beasts closed its eyes and lowered its head to the Merchant's feet. The Merchant grabbed Isabella and climbed onto its back. The Beasts roared as some Red soldiers backed away and then bounded towards the Teardrop Isles.

The second Beast fought off swords and spears until the Merchant and Isabella crossed the waters and galloped into the thick trees of the isles.

The three remaining men of the Merchant's fought fiercely and bravely, protecting the Merchant from the Red soldiers long enough for him to escape, but they finally succumbed and were cut down by the enemy.

With the Merchant and Isabella now clear of the Red Castle's shore, Pale Face was clear to bombard the Red Castle to the ground. But, just before he ordered the gunners to fire the cannons, he heard the high mast sailor screaming, 'Treason, treason.'

Pale Face, using his telescope, peered through one of the hatches. The pirate ships with the other half of the Merchant's fleet were on the horizon and approaching rapidly. And standing at the bow of the ship, commanding the fleet, stood the First Man, the traitor.

Pale Face turned to his men. 'Switch range, lock the floors and seal the belly,' he shouted. Word was passed from floor to floor. The doors now secured and the belly sealed, the long and short-range cannons aimed their guns at the approaching pirate ships engaged in battle with the Silvers.

'Fire,' Pale Face shouted. A tirade of cannon shots rained down on the pirates' ships. Meanwhile, the rogue Merchant's fleet kept Venus' long-range cannons pointed to the sea line, just as the First Man had planned.

The Red Castle, now relatively safe while the Merchant's ships were preoccupied, only had to overcome some fixed and short-range cannons to board Venus.

The Red soldiers streamed into the waters in vast numbers as the small cannons fired one after another, but undeterred, the Red soldiers kept coming. The guns were slowing the advancing troops but failed to stop them. The Red soldiers' commanders knew they had to seize Venus before the Merchant reached it, which drove them on.

The Dean stood high up on the hill, watching the events unfold. He smiled and took a sip of wine.

Chapter 67

The Red King slowly got to his feet, using the nearby wall to assist him. He coughed as he surveyed the room. The black smoke had cleared, and the dead and injured were being removed by his staff. He stared at the massive hole in the wall and beyond to the blue sky outside.

He made his way over the rubble, looked down at the carnage and smiled. His soldiers were pouring onto Venus and about to take control of the main deck while more soldiers on the shoreline slaughtered the second Beast and opened the way to the Teardrop Isles. Nothing could stop them from crossing the water and hunting down the Merchant. There was nowhere for him to escape to.

Once the Red soldiers had taken Venus' main deck, they rushed and found a lever, the main target identified by the First Man. They circled it, and the strongest soldier amongst them pulled it. The gears turned, drawing the cannons back inside and closing the hatches. The remaining Red soldiers rushed to the fire floors and attacked the doors with axes. Although the wood layer on the doors quickly yielded, they could not puncture through the alloy metal layer beneath. Frustrated, they hurried to the belly but faced the same metal doors beneath the wood. Only the key could open them. The fire floor doors were now sealed, and Red soldiers waited outside each of them while Pale Face and his gunners waited inside. But the hatches could only be opened from the main deck – Pale Face and his men were locked inside and helpless to do anything.

The First Man stopped his advance towards the Merchant's fleet, attempting to herd them under his command. The pirates lined up their ships away from the shoreline to draw the Silver navy towards them and away from any ground support – thwarting any opportunity to retreat and regroup.

The Saharan and his Line guards kept the Silver Knights engaged in a series of attacks – slowly draining the resistance of the Silver defence and depleting their arrows and spears.

The Silver Arch Knight was sure there was only one way to survive this. It was obvious to him. Sooner or later, the Saharan would reach the top, which would be a devastating blow. The Saharan's reputation was formidable, and no one fought like him. The Silver Arch Knight knew that attacking the Saharan on his way up – as the slope increased – gave the Silver defence the highland advantage over him, but if they waited any longer, they could lose the Archers' Towers, the Silver Kingdom's last line of defence.

The Line guards had to be stopped now. The Silver Knights had to change their strategy and meet the Saharan in a face-to-face survival battle.

The Silver Arch Knight drew his sword and held it aloft. 'Line up for attack!'

Chapter 68

The cannons of the battling pirates' and Silvers' ships echoed on the horizon as the First Man stood proudly aboard Venus which was now it was under his control.

'Have you taken control of the fire floors?' the First Man asked a Red soldier.

The Red soldier shook his head. 'No. We couldn't. The floors are sealed with steel doors just like the belly.'

The First Man's eyes widened. 'What?' This was something he hadn't planned for.

'What would you have us do?'

The First Man drummed his finger on a rail. 'Stay at the doors. Sooner or later, we will have the key.' He looked across at the Red Castle and slowly shook his head. 'Prima,' he whispered. He took out his telescope and scanned the bay. The bodies of Red soldiers and the Merchant's men littered the sand as blood-red water, ladened with more dead, lapped the shore. He viewed the shattered Red Castle with its black flags fluttering in the breeze. The injured crawled across the land while the Red soldiers continued their siege of The Teardrop Isles. He brought his telescope back around and stared into the Red Castle.

'Who are they?' he asked one of the Red soldiers, pointing at the Royal Anger Slayers. 'I've never seen them before.'

'They are men of Royal Anger,' the soldier said. 'The Red King declared Royal Anger, and they carried it out. They are called Slayers.'

The First Man frowned again. 'What is Royal Anger? What are Slayers?'

'The Red King ruined the castle, and the Slayers killed everyone in the royal court or threw them in the dungeons. He even killed the Minister when he tried to stop him.' The Red soldier lowered his head.

'And Prima? Where is Prima?' The First Man grabbed the Red soldier and shook him. 'Where is Prima?'

'I don't know. Only the royal guards are spared. She must be k … killed or in the dungeons.'

The First Man let him go and turned to the pirates he had with him. 'Ready three small boats and pack them with your best men. We are going in. We are going to the Red Castle.' He glared at the men as they stared at him. 'Now!'

Chapter 69

The Merchant made his way through the Teardrop Isles. Some were close enough to be crossed from one to another. He rode the Beast with Isabella holding him tightly, crossing the narrow waterways. He desperately wanted to reach the last isle and, from there, the open sea, from which he could get to Venus.

He stopped the Beast and made it kneel. 'Come on,' he said to Isabella as he hopped to the ground.

'Where are we going?' she asked as she took his hand and stepped down from the Beast.

'I will hide you.'

'What?' she snapped.

He took hold of her and kissed her gently on her forehead. 'I must sneak to the last isle and check it before we step on it. I don't hear any of my cannons firing. If my gunners didn't bombard the Red Castle, it must be because they couldn't. I am afraid Venus is taken.'

'And what are we going to do then?' She hugged him. 'Where would we go?'

The Merchant held her at arm's length. 'We will get back on Venus. But I will have to go alone first. Trust me. I will hide you well, and I will not be long. There is no other way to do this. I must go and check.' Isabella nodded, and the pair embraced.

Chapter 70

The First Man stood at the front of the boat, the other two vessels close behind, and slowly glided through the waterways between the Teardrop Isles. He intended to go around the isles, reach an off-site point of the shore, make his way unnoticed into the Red Castle, and then search for Prima.

He couldn't afford to waste time fighting the Slayers onshore or at the gates and, therefore, would have to sneak in with his men. He knew how and had become adept at it. He had never been caught all the times he had crept into the Red Castle to see Prima, his love.

They rowed slowly and as quietly as the task would permit, not wanting to alert anyone, especially the Merchant. The First Man fixed his eyes ahead on the dense treeline and shrubs as they passed near the isles. He knew that the Merchant would be close by, and if they crossed paths, they would have to fight, and though he had the pirates with him, and he was a skilled fighter, it was still a great risk.

'Faster, row a little faster,' he whispered.

Chapter 71

Deep inside the Teardrop Isles, the Merchant had hidden Isabella high up in the branches of a tree.

He allowed himself a peek over the Beast's back as he crossed the final Teardrop Isle. Red soldiers lined up at the shoreline – the one that led to the open sea and the closest isle to Venus. Though he had the Beast, he had no plan to attack. The cannon hatches were closed, and therefore, Venus had been taken.

He knew he couldn't defeat them in a single attack, so he had to be patient. He would wait for as long as it took and ambush them one by one as they came for him.

Chapter 72

The wait was unbearable to everyone in the caves. The people were tense, nervous, and afraid. They sat tight, lost in their thoughts and worry, except the Mute. He had his eyes fixed on one person. One face. One girl.

He gazed at her as she sat quietly across the cave – a girl he had always adored. He didn't know her name, but she was bewitching. Although her eyes captivated him, and her long hair flowed elegantly behind her beautiful face, it was her smile that truly captured him. She was untainted by the dust of poverty – her purity entranced him, and he had fallen deeply in love with her. She was a couple of years older than him, and even with his confidence, wits and charm, he had never dared to approach her, fearing her rejection. He had never dared to express his feelings to her, but he had enough hope to dream. He imagined how it would feel to be with her – in love, happy, intimate, the places they would go to, the laughs they would share, the gifts he would shower her with. These dreams weren't real except for one – he owned a pearl, a gift he would love to give her. Divers from the far east risked their lives in pursuit of these pearls – diving deep into the sea and denying themselves air for a long time to possess one. He had purchased the finest he could find and kept it hidden in his pocket for years, never mustering enough courage to give it to her.

'What are you waiting for,' he thought. 'This could be the last night of your life. Give her the pearl. Make it count.'

He summoned his nerve, stood, and walked towards the orphans huddled together at the cave's end – she was an orphan herself and their leader and caretaker – and sat before her. He fished inside his pocket and pulled out the pearl wrapped in soft orange cloth, and as she gazed at him, he stretched out his hand and opened his palm.

Chapter 73

The Red King sat on his throne, staring through the wide cannon hole that had split open his castle.

One of the commanding Red guards entered and stopped before the Red King. 'Your Grace, the Merchant hasn't emerged from the Teardrop Isles. What shall we do?'

'Did we get the gold?' the King asked.

'No, your Highness, the Belly is sealed in steel.'

'Did anyone get the key or at least know where it is?' the Red King said.

'He must have it, your Grace.'

The King glowered at the guard. 'Then send our soldiers into the isles to capture the Merchant. Capture him and bring me the key. Find the Merchant and bring him to me alive. I want to kill him myself.'

'At your command, my King.' The Red Guard saluted and turned to leave.

'And the Silvers,' the King bellowed, 'have we taken their kingdom?'

'No, your Grace, they are putting up stubborn resistance. The Saharan is attempting to seize the Arched Towers, and the pirate ships are engaging with the Silver fleet at sea as we speak. Our navy is managing to keep the Silvers away from Venus, but until we have defeated their fleet, we are unable to invade their shoreline and seize the Silver Kingdom.' The Red King balled his hands into fists. 'There is something more, your Grace …'

The Red King grunted. 'What?'

'I will send in our men as you requested, but the Merchant still has the Beast with him. He rode it into the isles.'

'Send your men at dusk. The Beasts are at their weakest then.'

'Would he remain there that long?' the Red Guard asked.

'If he has to.'

The Red King stood and moved across to the rubble in front of the hole in the wall. 'Send for the artist. I want him to paint me here on the throne, in front of this rubble.'

The Red Guard frowned.

'It will serve as a reminder to the court of our struggle when we have secured victory.'

Chapter 74

The girl sighed. 'It's almost night. Why is it taking so long?' she asked the Mute. Although he couldn't hear her, he understood.

She smiled at him and gazed at the pearl he had gifted her. She had never had this kind of attention before, and no one had ever given her such a precious object. She looked deep into his eyes, and a feeling she had never felt before coursed through her.

A Silver Guard appeared at the cave's entrance – weary and bruised holding onto his dented shield. 'Get ready to leave,' he shouted.

The people cheered, but the Silver Guard held up his hand. 'You are not going back to the village,' he said. The chattering amongst the people receded. 'We can barely hold the shore,' he continued. 'We cannot resist the Saharan for much longer. You must flee. The kingdom … the Silver Kingdom …' He took a deep breath. '… Is almost lost!'

Chapter 75

The First Man finally reached the dungeons, deep beneath the castle, where no sunlight penetrated and darkness reigned. The wall, the floor and everything inside them was painted black. A blackness swallowed any light that strayed near.

The pirates quickly killed the few remaining guards as the First Man stood at the foot of the stairs, his feet chilled by this place. He felt afraid – not the fear of battle nor the awful sight of the grave-like dungeons, it was the fear of what he might find down there in this unforgiving place. 'What if she's hurt?' He thought. 'What if she died …?' He hardly dared think about it.

He slowly made his way through the dungeons and past prisoners locked up in cells – their chains rattling rhythmically as they called out for mercy.

He continued, passing more wretched souls – their pleading more plaintive as he grew close to them. He reached another corridor – even colder, darker and more suffocating than the others. Something grabbed his attention, and he edged towards it. It was a well – circular and made of stone – but without a bucket or rope to draw water. He knew that the Red King was creative in torturing his enemies. The well had to be much worse than any of those dungeons.

'I will look there first,' he thought.

He searched for a light, grabbed a flaming torch from its holder, and crept nearer. As the light illuminated the edge of the well, he gasped. A heavy iron web sealed the top, and within this, blood-covered human limbs littered the floor. As he reached the well and the torch shone more light on this horrid scene, he realised that the limbs, arms and legs were human bodies piled on each other. A hand – a woman's, caught his attention, and he dropped the torch and fell to his knees. The hand wore a ring. The ring that he had placed on her finger. It was Prima's hand.

'Oh, Prima,' he cried. He picked up the torch and took hold of her hand. It was cold and devoid of life. Lowering his head, he gently kissed it as tears flowed from him. 'Prima is dead,' he thought. 'Oh, Prima! The blade must have been cold, oh my dear Prima, my sweet helpless Prima, they have cut you to death. You must have been scared. How couldn't they have shown mercy? Did you call for me? You must have looked your slayer in the eyes and silently begged him to spare your life. You must have trembled and shaken. You must have felt cold, Prima, and I couldn't take you in my arms and warm you. You must have been so afraid, and the pain, oh, the pain you've felt! The blade must have been cold as it cut through your warm heart. Oh, Prima. I am sorry I wasn't there. I am sorry I failed you.'

He slumped to the ground beside the well, and still holding her hand tightly, he sobbed.

Chapter 76

The Mute took his mother's arm as they left the cave and signed. 'Where will we go?'

'I don't know, but we have to run now,' she signed back.

He stood still. 'It is stupid. We are fooling ourselves if we think we can leave the Silver Kingdom alive. Even if we did, the Red guards would hunt us down. The Red King has always wanted to wipe us out. Where else can we go? The lands around our kingdom are his. All the kingdoms are his.'

'What's going on?' one of the old men said.

The Mute's mother turned to him. 'My son is saying we are doomed, and the Reds will kill us whether we stay in the caves or run.'

'We have to try,' the old man said. 'There is no other way. There is nothing else we can do.'

'There is,' the Mute signed, and his mother told the others.

'Hurry up, all of you back there,' the Silver soldier said.

'Wait a minute!' the girl, or Pearl, as the Mute now called her, shouted.

'There is one thing we can do to get out of this,' the Mute signed again – his mother relayed the words to the crowd, who edged closer.

The Mute continued to sign to his mother, and she translated. 'If we stay, we die. If we run, they will hunt us down. The Red King will be merciless with any he captures. Let's not fool ourselves. If the Silver Kingdom is going to be defeated, it shouldn't happen until the last one of us is dead. I say we fight. I say we make this the night where old men, women and children fought to the last. I say we lay down our candles and pick up our swords.'

'Well said, young fella,' the Silver soldier commented. 'But even if you gathered your courage to fight, there are insufficient swords and spears for all of you. Our weapons are in the hands of our dead soldiers downhill.'

The Mute signalled, 'I know where to get weapons. The weapons that are waiting for us at the shore —the weapons the Merchant put there – are the ones we will hold in our hands. We will climb down to the beach from around the hill to get there faster, and our mothers will stay here, and they will beat the war drums for every pirate and Red soldier to hear.'

Chapter 77

The pirates had almost wiped out the Silver fleet, and only a few of the Merchant's men were still alive and fighting. The Saharan took out one defence after another while moving uphill, getting closer and closer to the Silver Arched Towers. Only a few tired Silver soldiers remained. They could not beat the Saharan or defend and hold the shore much longer. Sooner or later, the pirates and the Red soldiers would swarm into the Silver Kingdom.

All those thoughts ran through the mind of the Silver King as he saw the last of the Silver guards lining up for battle. He paused and waited. He didn't send the soldiers downhill immediately for another attack against the Saharan and his men. He was reluctant, for this was not just another wave of attack. It was the last.

'My King,' one of the Silver soldiers said.

'What is it now?' the Silver King replied.

'The villagers want to fight. They've brought swords and want to fight.'

'What? We don't have any more armour for them.'

'They know, my King,' the Silver soldier said, 'but they are determined to fight the enemy to the death.'

The Silver King looked behind the soldier at his people, with the Mute at the head of them, holding the Merchant's blue swords and spears in their hands. The Mute stepped closer to the King. Then, standing astride a rock, he brought the point of the blade down as hard as he could, piercing it.

'We know you have no armour,' he signed as his twin brother spoke, 'but we also know that the armour would not stop the Reds from stabbing our hearts. The only way to stop them is to fight them.'

The Silver King stepped forward and pushed the Mute backwards away from the rock. 'Go! Run away. There is no place for you in battle. It is our doom. Run all of you. Such a battle can't be won by a bunch of old men, women, and children.'

The Silver King grasped the sword's handle and attempted to pull it free from the rock. It stubbornly remained. He pulled harder, but the blade held firm. He tried again and again. Finally, exhausted, he let go of the sword and stepped back. The Mute jumped on the rock and then signed as his twin said his words, 'Yes, we might die. Some of us might die if we fight, but if we don't, all of us will. We march with you bravely because we also know that it is not the weapons in our hands nor the armour on our chests that our enemy fears, but it's what's in our hearts.' He patted his chest. 'Brave hearts kill more enemies than sharp swords. When they see how brave we are and that we do not fear death, they will know how dearly we value our land.' He looked at the King. 'Yes, we are a bunch of old men, women, and children in your eyes, and no, we don't have armour or horses, but you know that we are your last chance. We are all you have. And we are walking to battle.' The Mute took hold of the sword and easily pulled it from the stone. He held up the blade as everyone cheered.

Chapter 78

The Reds, weapons drawn, waited on the Teardrop Isle and kept their eyes on the thick line of trees, ready to confront the Merchant if he appeared. Their leader looked through his telescope at the Red Castle's shoreline, waiting for the signal to mount a double assault and attack the Merchant from both ends. An attack flag was finally waved, and he turned to his men. 'March on,' he commanded his men, and they moved forward into the thick forest.

At the same moment, the Saharan signalled all the onshore forces to the borderline as a huge number of Silvers lined uphill, ready to attack.

The lines of Red soldiers moved steadily through the trees, not knowing where the Merchant was. They were apprehensive, lacking morale and unsure if they could defeat the Merchant, for all the soldiers who had previously been sent after him had never come back. They had heard screaming from within the forest, but none had returned. Nonetheless, they moved forward while pirates and Red soldiers onboard Venus kept their eyes on the Isle and closely watched them as they disappeared behind its deep, dense treeline.

Chapter 79

The artist's hands shook as he unsteadily painted the Red King, who sat quietly on his throne in front of the rubble. It was difficult to ignore the sounds of the battles going on outside, and he flinched whenever the sound of the ships' cannons or the royal guards' swords got closer to the throne hall.

The Red King hadn't moved. Still and gloomy, he looked at the painter as if he didn't care or worry about anything. He looked like he was in a deep meditation – his eyes staring into the darkness.

The artist dropped the brush and quickly turned as the First Man burst into the room. None of the royal guards had been able to stop him. He had slaughtered them all.

The First Man stepped closer, his blood-covered sword hanging loosely in one hand while in the other, Prima's ring.

The Painter edged away and shrunk into one of the corners.

The First Man glanced at him. 'I am not here for you,' he said, turning his attention back to the King. The painter ran, stumbled, and, regaining his footing, fled the throne hall.

'Can you feel it?' the Red King said, still gazing into the distance. 'It is dark. Love lights you up, but the loss of love darkens you. Now it is dark and cold. It can bring the best or the worst out of you. My anger has now subsided.' He turned and looked at the First Man. 'You must feel the same.'

'You killed her!' The First Man gritted his teeth. 'You ordered your Slayers to kill her.' He wiped the tears from his eyes. 'She was too beautiful to die.'

The Red King sighed. 'Yes, I understand. You are travelling through the same darkness as I am.' The Red King stood, drew his sword, and opened his arms. 'Come. Let the might of our darkness meet on the edges of our blades.'

The First Man bolted across the room with his weapon raised high, and the Red King, wielding his own, met him midway as their swords crossed, clanged, and sparked.

Chapter 80

The pirates and Red soldiers aboard Venus kept their eyes on the Isle's treeline, waiting and hoping for the Red soldiers to emerge, having captured the Merchant and killed the Beast.

The trees shook, and screams could clearly be heard across the water, but after a long silence, the Merchant came crashing out of the trees on the Beast's back, with Isabella holding on to him tightly.

They leapt into the waters – the Beast quickly closing the distance from shore to vessel – and as the Beast reached the ship, it slowed, allowing the Merchant and Isabella to jump free and climb the bowline to the deck. Isabella gripped the Merchant as they reached the figurehead.

The pirate ships fired at the Beast, and the Red soldiers threw their spears at it, but the Beast was fierce and didn't fall quickly. The Merchant intended to use this precious time to reach the lever, unleash the cannons, and free his men.

As Isabella held on to Venus' figurehead, the Merchant raced across the main deck, killing any pirate or Red soldier that stood in his way. But there were too many, as one after another followed their fallen crewmates, the Merchant tired and couldn't reach the lever. He glanced across at his wife and grimaced as he felt a sword pierce his side.

Isabella cried out, and the Merchant dropped onto his knees, allowing his sword to fall from his grasp as blood spurted from the wound.

The pirates and soldiers surrounded the stricken Merchant and pointed their swords at the Merchant's throat. 'The key,' one of them demanded.

The Merchant glanced at his blood-covered shirt and then back to Isabella – her eyes filled with tears. The taste of blood filled his mouth, and he spat a mouthful of the viscous red fluid. His head swam, and he struggled for breath as he looked towards the slaughtered Beast – its body covered with arrows and spears – then back at his wife once more, still clinging tightly to the figurehead.

'All right,' the Merchant said, struggling to his feet. He staggered toward the figurehead as the pirates and soldiers watched on.

The Red King and the First Man had fought fiercely inside the Red Castle. The First Man, surprised by the strength of his foe – the King's first strike had almost brought him to his knees – had managed to recover and battle on, but he was tiring, and as the King met his sword again, the First Man was sent sprawling backwards onto the floor.

The Silvers raised their flags for one last battle with the Saharan and his men as the pirates' cannons shattered the last Silver ship. From his vantage point above, the Black family's Dean smiled.

The Merchant passed Isabella, briefly touching his wife's hand as he did so, and reached the far tip of the pole. He dropped down heavily and didn't move. The pirates and soldiers glanced between themselves as Isabella gasped, but then the Merchant moved, stretching his arms around Venus' face. He pressed the eyes of the figurehead, and the mouth opened, revealing two small gold daggers. The Merchant stood and, holding a blade in each hand, stretched out his arms. A hole on either side of the pole opened, and two gold shackles emerged, securing his feet to the figurehead. He closed his eyes and lifted his head. The waves around the ship stopped their incessant crashing against the vessel's side until the sea waters stilled. The pirates and soldiers mumbled as they looked at each other and then back to the Merchant.

Slowly at first, a small number of waves formed around the ships and as each one made its way towards Venus, they merged until they created a huge wave. Quicker and quicker it moved, gathering speed and size as it neared. Everyone stared at the wave that continued to grow in size and rapidly closed in on the ship. What made the wave even more unusual was that rather than approaching from the horizon, this wave was heading towards the ship's bow. It had formed sideways to shore. The wave hit Venus' figurehead, lifting the bow so high it came clear of the water and plunged the stern so low that it sank into the sea. The pirates and the Red soldiers desperately grasped onto the ropes to stop themselves from falling off the back of the ship. Those who were not lost and had found something to cling to gazed in awe at the Merchant standing on Venus' figurehead, rising high above them all.

Isabella clung to the pole at the end of the figurehead. While everyone struggled to stay on board, the Merchant stood still, his feet anchored to the figurehead by the shackles and spikes protruding from his shoes. The figurehead's mouth opened as blood dripped from its eyes, the same blood that covered the Merchant's hands.

Thunder roared in the skies, and huge raindrops fell, whipping the wind into a frenzy. As the wave continued to travel towards the stern, the bow dropped. The Merchant leapt through the air and over the pirates' heads, landing behind them as they helplessly slid towards the figurehead.

With the Mute beside the Silver King, the Silvers stormed downhill, screaming their battle cries, their swords held high as the mothers beat the war drums above.

The First Man's energy was almost spent. He had been unable to lay a sword on the Red King as he lifted his weapon up high for a final time.

The Merchant moved quickly, attacking the helpless pirates and the Red soldiers – who could not defend themselves – and slit their throats one by one with his gold daggers. The shouting and screaming subsided as the last pirates were washed from the deck, leaving the way clear to the lever. The Merchant hurried across to it and pulled.

Down on the fire floor, Pale Face jumped to his feet as the hatches opened. 'Load,' he shouted. His men quickly leapt into action and primed the cannons. 'Switch range,' Pale Face commanded.

At the same time, the Silvers stormed down the hill and met the Saharan lines, slamming into each other. Many fell at the point of their enemy's swords and spears. The Silver King spotted the Saharan in battle. Slashing his way past the soldiers, he confronted him, raising his blade above the giant. The Saharan, anticipating the attack, sidestepped the sword and plunged his dagger into the King's neck. The King dropped to his knees and then onto his face. The Saharan roared, but as he turned in triumph, the Mute jumped onto his back and plunged his own dagger deep into the throat of the Saharan. The Mute stepped away from him, the blade pushed down into the hilt as copious amounts of blood pumped from the Saharan's severed artery. The Saharan groaned, stumbled backwards and fell with a huge crash onto the floor. The Mute stepped closer and looked down at him as the Saharan's lifeless eyes stared back.

More pirates and Red soldiers climbed aboard Venus to fight the Merchant, but one by one, he slaughtered them as the wave pushed the pirate ships further away from Venus until they were unable to board her.

As soon as the cannons were in place, Pale Face shouted, 'Fire.'

Venus' long-range cannons pounded the Red Castle and Red soldiers in a terrific bombardment. The Red soldiers scattered in all directions.

The surviving Silvers headed back uphill, leaving Venus to finish the battle. The short-range cannons were turned on the pirate ships sending them to the seabed while the Merchant cleared the main deck of the enemy.

The Dean, overlooking the battle, screamed and threw his champagne flute against a rock.

Cannonballs crashed into the walls of the Red Castle, shaking the ancient structure to its foundations. The Red King stumbled and dropped his sword. Seizing his opportunity, the First Man barrelled into the Red King, crashing with such force that the momentum carried the pair through the crumbling walls. They plummeted downwards to their deaths.

Pale Face ordered the cannons to fire again and again. Switching ranges and commanding the cannons like a master gunner in a symphony of gunfire that continued for the rest of the night, flattening the Red Castle to the ground.

It was dawn when the cannons stopped firing – the mist and the smoke from the barrage screening Venus from the shoreline.

The remaining Red soldiers on shore searched desperately for survivors through the debris. They came across a woman's hand, covered in blood – the rest of her beneath the fallen masonry and quickly dug her free. The soldiers were overwhelmed to discover it was the Queen, shaken but not badly injured.

They helped her to stand, and the Queen, her eyes full of tears, surveyed the wreckage of her once mighty kingdom. Virtually nothing of the Red Castle remained. She sobbed as the soldiers led her past countless bodies and severed limbs scattered everywhere in this blood-soaked land. They helped her towards the shore, and she stared at the horizon. Venus was gone. Most of the Merchant's ships had vanished, leaving only the stricken vessels floundering in the sea while dozens of pirate ships lay partly submerged in the blue waters. No one had seen him sail away, and no one was sure if he ever did.

With slow, trembling steps, the Queen, leaning on the Red guards for support, climbed the hill to gain a better view. She looked again, but the horizon was clear, and there was no sign of the Merchant or his fleet. The waters beyond the battleground were empty.

Chapter 81

The storm still raged outside. "What happened?" the sailor asked as the waves slammed against the lighthouse.

The old keeper shrugged. "Some say the Merchant sailed away into the distance after destroying the remaining pirate ships. Some say he escaped and hid with his love Isabella on some island away from the rest of the world." The old keeper laughed. "Some believe that he sailed up to the skies or down to the deep. No one knows for certain where the Merchant and his fleet went. But everyone knows, for sure, that whoever has seen, met, or heard about the Merchant will never forget him or the magnificence of his fleet."

"What about the rest?" The sailor widened his eyes. "What happened to them?"

"The Mute became the new and youngest ever silver king," the old keeper said. "After the Silvers were almost wiped out in the battle, he married the girl he loved and made peace with the Reds. As for the Blacks – or what remained of them and the Dean – they returned to their shadows." The old keeper turned and looked outside as the wind whistled through the lighthouse.

"And the Queen?" The sailor said. "What happened to her?"

The old keeper sighed, still looking outside and deep into the horizon. "Ah, the Queen?"

"Yes. The Queen."

The old keeper turned and stood before the sailor. "The Queen remained there all day. From dawn till dusk, she searched the horizon for any sign of the Merchant. And when the night finally fell, she commanded her guards to bring her a torch. She held it high all night for the Merchant to find his way back to shore if he was at sea trying to return. Or at least she believed that seeing her light might soften his heart." The old keeper sighed again, then continued. "The longer the Merchant was gone, the wider the hardship spread. Poverty, illnesses, and starvation shaded the lands. The darker it got across the lands, the more guilty the Queen felt. The more guilty she felt, the longer she stood on that hill holding the light for the Merchant to return. Day after day, night after night, month after month, and year after year."

"Yet, he never returned?"

The old keeper shook his head. "No. Eventually, she was unable to hold the torch all night. They erected a copper statue holding a torch that would stand atop the hill and be lit every night. She grew old and sick, and gathering her knights, she made them promise to keep the torch lit every night. They pledged to travel far and wide, lighting their torches. She passed away, but her knights kept their promise. Over ice, grass, and sand across the world, they kept the torches lit. Over mountains, hills, and islands. We rode horses, sailed ships, climbed rocks, and kept our pledge. We kept the light. People started to call us the lightkeepers, and when we started building houses, they called us the lighthouse keepers." The sailor gaped at the old keeper, and he smiled. "Yes, the lighthouse keepers," he said.

"You are one of them? You are a knight?" the sailor said as the storm outside roared louder and louder. The old man smiled again and nodded.

Before night fell, the sailor stepped out of the lighthouse while the storm still raged and pulled the collar of his coat up higher.

"Are you waiting for him?" the sailor recalled asking the old keeper as he stopped walking and looked up to the lighthouse. He saw the shadow of the old keeper standing next to the glass window and remembered his words.

"Him, or anyone like him," the old keeper had replied. "Anyone who stands for what he stood for may be him. Someone who fights for what he fought for, who defends what he believed, could be him. Anyone who has goodness in his heart is him." The old keeper had pulled a lever, a chain rattled, and the large lamp lit up bright.

The sailor heard the Queen's voice inside his head. "Light it up," she commanded, and he saw it. He saw the light beaming from one place on the horizon to another. The rain continued falling, and the sailor grasped his bag and felt inside. He pulled out a book that was not his. A book he somehow recognised. A book that once belonged to the Merchant. He looked up at the lighthouse once more and saw the old keeper's shadow standing next to the lamp, but as the lightning flashed, the old keeper was gone. Yet still, his words echoed in the sailor's head.

"And now you've heard my story, judge it. Judge every person, every intention, and every action. Judge it, for one's judgment, reveals nothing but oneself. What would you have done? Who would you have helped? Who would you have stopped? Judge it, for out there, on those lands, there will always be a Red King. There will always be the Queen. There will always be the Blacks, the pirates, and the brave Mute, but there won't always be the Merchant. As for us, the light-keepers, we wait. We keep the light throughout the night. We don't watch the world burn. We keep the light so that good can return."

The sailor turned to the sea and saw the light of a ship close to shore.

He raised his hand while holding the book tightly as he recalled the old keeper's last words to him,

"And now, you have to choose. Before you take another step, choose. Choose a home or a ship."

Inspirations

Music

The Queen holds the light:
Audioslave - Like a Stone

Royal Anger:
Ciara - Paint it Black

General theme & end battle:
Kronos Quartet - Requiem For A Dream

The Knights' Pledge:
Clocks & Clouds - Requiem For A Dream

The Keeper and the Sailor - from Beginning to End:
Lorne Balfe feat. Madeline Bell - Assassin's Creed Revelations

The Merchant - Jai Kai - the rope:
Zack Hemsey - Mind Heist

Prima wondering at night:
Hooverphonic - Mad About You (Orchestra Version)

Stories & Legacies

Zheng Hu

Santa Isabella

Arthur

Cinderella

Hunchback of Notre Dame

Red Riding Hood

Structures

Statue of Liberty

Lighthouses

Edited By

JV Author Services
JVAS Team
John & Vicky Regan
Instagram @jvauthorservices

Cover Design

Larraine Rowney
Instagram @flossdesign2022

Contact Author

www.ukinkers.com

Email: contact@ukinkers.com
Instagram: @sherif_hotabiy
Tiktok: @sherifelhotabiy
Twitter: @sherifelhotabiy

Facebook page: Sherif EL-Hotabiy

#The_Merchant_the_Novel